SWEET OBSESSION

A SWEET COVE MYSTERY BOOK 16

J. A. WHITING

To hear about new books and book sales, please sign up for my
mailing list at:
www.jawhiting.com

❀ Created with Vellum

For my family with love

ngie Roseland worked the counter in her newly-opened, bake shop-café located in the Sweet Cove Museum at the southern end of the pretty, Massachusetts seacoast town. The museum, only a few blocks from the shops and restaurants of Coveside, was one of the finest of its size housing collections of American art, photography, maritime art, Native American art, and Asian art, as well as an expansive collection of textiles.

A welcoming foyer led into the airy atrium with a soaring glass roof allowing plenty of light into the space in the middle of the museum where four brick buildings radiated out from the center leading visitors into the galleries and studios.

This was Angie's second café and it was set up in

a corner of the atrium where it had proven very popular with the visitors who were happy to sit at the tables to enjoy delicious bakery items, coffees and teas, breads, soups, salads, and sandwiches throughout the day.

Rectangular planters filled with summer flowers and greenery were placed in a way that divided the café from the rest of the space and gave people a place to relax before or after their visits to the galleries. Open for only a month, the food and beverages had been a huge hit with the patrons, and the Trustees were more than pleased with the successful addition of Angie's café, The Sweet Dreams Bake Shop II.

To get the shop up and running, Angie had the help of her three sisters, the family friend, Victor Finch, her shop manager, Louisa, and several new employees including another family friend, Orla O'Brien who had been hired to work at the café in the family's Victorian mansion in the center of Sweet Cove.

With all the work of organizing and setting up the new shop and running her bakery-café in the town center, Angie had another reason that contributed to her feelings of exhaustion and fatigue … she'd just completed her third month of pregnancy. Not only had she felt tired all the time, but she'd suffered from morning sickness that had lasted all day long.

Angie's fraternal twin sister, Jenna, was also expecting a baby and their due dates were only days apart in February. Because Jenna, too, had morning sickness and fatigue, the sisters worked hard to encourage and support each other through the difficult three months. Although Angie and Jenna were twins, many people didn't believe it at first since Jenna was taller with brunette hair and Angie was shorter and had honey-blond hair.

One day, an older customer came up to the counter and told them that if they thought feeling sick and dragging themselves through the day was bad, then just wait until those kids are born. "Once those kids come into the world, you'll never have another day of peace."

Angie and Jenna had exchanged looks with one another and when the customer moved away from the counter to find a table, the twins couldn't suppress a fit of giggles.

"Why on earth would she say that to us?" Jenna asked. "We can't exactly go back in time and change our decision to have babies."

"I guess she's warning us that the future is

bleak," Angie smiled. "We'd better enjoy ourselves during the next six months because after that it's all over."

Now that their first trimesters were done, both sisters were feeling much better and had a lot more energy. Things at the new bake shop were falling into place and the job of running two cafés was becoming routine for Angie.

Louisa, the hard-working manager, was in her late twenties, had the body of a dancer, beautiful eyes, and long, black hair with the ends dyed blue. "Did you hear about that explosion in Solana Village? There was a package left on the victim's front porch and when she went to pick it up, it exploded."

"I did hear." Angie was making a protein smoothie for a customer. "The woman will be okay, right? She was hurt, but her injuries aren't life-threatening, are they?"

"Thankfully, she's supposed to recover." Louisa cut a slice from a coconut custard pie for one of the patrons. "What kind of a nut would do that to someone?"

"Do you think the injured woman knows the person who left the device on the porch?" Angie asked.

"The police don't know yet. It's being investigated." Louisa carried a piece of pie and a cup of coffee to a man at one of the tables.

With the back of her hand, Angie pushed a strand of her dark blond hair from her eyes and noticed someone striding across the floor of the atrium towards her. A smile moved over her mouth as Sweet Cove Chief of Police Phillip Martin approached the counter.

Tall and stocky with a bit of gray showing at the temples, Chief Martin was in his mid-fifties, was a life-long resident of the town, and had known the Roseland sisters' grandmother for years. The four Roselands had inherited something special from their nana ... each one had a certain skill ... a skill that would fall under the category of paranormal ability.

A very distant relative of the Roselands had left her Sweet Cove Victorian mansion to Angie and when the family moved from Boston to the seaside town, it was then that their abilities began to emerge. Three of the sisters were more accepting of their unusual skills than the fourth sibling was, but they were all learning to manage what they were able to do.

Chief Martin often called on the Roselands to

assist with difficult cases, something their grand-mother had done for the police many years ago.

"Hi," Angie greeted the chief and handed him a mug of black coffee. "What brings you to the museum?"

"Well, *you* do, actually." Chief Martin took a long swallow from the cup.

A bit of a shiver ran down Angie's back and her eyes narrowed as she watched the man's face. "Did you come in to see how I was doing?" she asked, knowing very well that the chief had a different reason for his visit.

Chief Martin smiled. "How are you doing? Everything going well?"

"Everything's great. I don't know why I was so worried about opening a second bake shop. It's all running very smoothly."

"Glad to hear it." The chief eyed Angie's abdomen for a second. The baby wasn't showing yet. "And the little one? How's she doing?"

"Gigi's fine. I don't feel her moving or fluttering yet." Angie's blue eyes sparkled. "The doctor said it's too soon."

Almost a year ago, the Roseland sisters were involved in helping Chief Martin with a serious case which Jenna sensed might cause harm or death to

Angie, and incredibly, the spirit of Angie's future daughter was able to provide warnings that helped keep her mother safe. The little girl's name would be Genevieve, and Angie and her husband, Josh, would call her Gigi.

"You're still feeling better?" The chief was aware of Angie's and Jenna's bouts of morning sickness.

"Yes. That's all behind me now. Jenna's over it, too." Angie nodded and chuckled. "And not a moment too soon for either of us."

"Good." The chief seemed a little uneasy.

Angie kept her voice low. "What's up? Is something wrong?"

"Nothing's wrong." Chief Martin replied with a little too much gusto.

"Spill it," Angie told the man. "I've known you for quite a while. I can tell when something's bothering you."

The chief sighed. "Can you sit down for a minute? Do you have some time?"

Angie went over to speak with Louisa for a moment, and then she walked out from behind the counter and led the chief to an empty table away from the other patrons.

Chief Martin set his mug on the tabletop. "Have you heard about the trouble down in Solana?"

"The explosive device? It was on someone's porch?"

The chief gave a quick nod. "Yes, that incident. There's been another one as well. It was found this morning ... a package in a mailbox."

"Was anyone hurt by it?" Angie's eyes clouded.

"No. The person became suspicious of the package when he spotted it so he called the police to come and check it out. It was set to explode when someone opened it." The chief's brow furrowed from concern.

Angie's heart dropped when she recognized the look on his face. She knew the family was about to be drawn into the investigation. "Is there something we can do to help?"

"I was hoping so. The chief in Solana Village, Benny Peterson, and I are friends. He's asked me to consult on the case. He's concerned this is going to get bigger, that trouble is going to spread its wings over his town. Their police force is smaller than ours. He's very worried."

"Why does he think the problem is going to get bigger?" Angie asked.

"Two bombs in one day," Chief Martin explained. "He doesn't think that will be the end of it."

"He thinks more people will receive bombs?" Angie leaned forward a little.

The chief nodded. "Nothing like this has happened in Sweet Cove. Yet. My friend, Benny, thinks we need to be proactive on this. He's worried the bomber will spread the trouble to a number of other towns."

"Why does he think that?"

"Benny lived in New York earlier in his career. It was a small city. Something similar happened there and the guy responsible for the explosives didn't keep his criminal activities isolated to one town."

"Was the perpetrator caught back then?" Angie's heart began to pound.

"No."

A chill ran over Angie's skin. "Does your friend think the same person could be responsible for the past explosives in New York and the ones happening now in Solana?"

"Unlikely." Chief Martin raised his mug to his lips. "But not impossible, I suppose. Right now, the main goal is finding the person who left explosives in Solana and keeping people safe."

"Are there any clues?"

"Not a whole lot." The chief shook his head. "Any chance some of you might be able to help us out?"

Angie tilted her head to the side and made eye contact with the man. "Have we ever refused you?"

"There's always a first time."

"No, there isn't." Shaking her head, Angie added kindly, "At least not with us there isn't. If you need us, we'll be right there by your side. Just like always."

I t was early evening when Chief Martin came by the Victorian to talk with the family about the new case. When they heard the chief would be coming to visit, Euclid, the huge, orange, Maine Coon cat and Circe, the sweet black cat with a dot of white on her chest, sat in the foyer on the bottom step of the staircase waiting for the doorbell to ring.

The foyer of the Victorian had gleaming hard-wood floors and high ceilings with a shimmering crystal chandelier hung over the center of the space. A large ornate wooden staircase led from the foyer to the second floor landing and there was a carved rectangular, cherrywood table that stood in the middle of the foyer with a large cut glass

vase filled with flowers. Rugs of muted cream, cran-
berry, and green colors were placed here and there
over the floor. The mansion was perfectly decorated with period furniture, wallpaper, lamps,
antiques, and mirrors and entering the home was
like stepping back into an era of elegance and fine
taste.

Ellie, the middle sister born in-between the
twins and the youngest Roseland, had long blond
hair, was tall and slim, efficient, smart, and well-
mannered. She ran a popular bed and breakfast inn
out of the mansion that received rave reviews from
the guests. She was also the sister who wished the
family's special skills would disappear and never
return.

When the bell rang, Ellie was in the dining room
putting out the evening snacks and drinks for the
guests and she hurried to open the door for the
chief.

"Evening, Ellie." The chief stepped inside and
Euclid and Circe padded over to the man for some
petting just as the other family members came to
greet him.

"We have tea and coffee set up in the sunroom,"
Jenna announced.

Leaning on his cane, Mr. Finch carried a small

tray with a fruit and custard pie on it made by Angie. "We can't have a meeting without something to eat."

"Courtney will be home in a little while," Angie informed the chief. "She's at the candy shop." Courtney and Mr. Finch were co-owners of the Sweet Cove Candy Shop in the center of town.

As Angie, Finch, Jenna, and Chief Martin headed for the sunroom with the two cats running ahead, Ellie held back. "I need to get some things done in the kitchen. Maybe I'll join you later."

"Are you sure you don't want to sit in on the meeting from the beginning instead of coming in at the tail end?" Angie thought it would be more helpful if Ellie heard what the chief had to say from the start.

"I guess I could." Ellie fiddled with the end of a long strand of her hair. "If you think that would be better."

Angie nodded and gave her reluctant sister an encouraging smile.

When they had poured cups of tea and coffee and Finch had sliced the tart and passed the small plates around to everyone, they all took seats and the chief cleared his throat and began his tale of the Solana Village case.

"As you all know, Solana has had a couple of

incidents recently where an explosive device was left on a porch and another one inside a mailbox. The first bomb exploded when it was picked up by the woman living in the house. The second bomb was diffused after the owner discovered the suspicious package in his mailbox."

"Has anything like this happened in Solana previously?" Finch asked as he pushed his black frame glasses up to the bridge of his nose.

"Not to my knowledge," Chief Martin said.

"Is there some connection between the people who live in the two targeted homes?" Angie questioned. Euclid sat on the floor next to Angie's chair watching her eat the tart.

"There doesn't seem to be."

"Any fingerprints?" Jenna had her long brown hair held back in a braid that rested over one shoulder.

"None."

"Are there any security cameras located at those houses?" Finch asked. "Some homeowners have installed cameras at the front and back of their properties."

Circe snuggled next to Mr. Finch on the sofa resting her head against his leg.

"Unfortunately, these homeowners didn't have

any cameras at their homes." Chief Martin finished his piece of pie and Finch cut him a second slice. "The neighbors didn't notice anything or anyone suspicious nearby. No one has reported seeing a delivery truck or a passenger car parked close to the houses."

"Could someone have approached the homes from the rear?" Ellie's question caused her sisters to look at her with surprise. Often during a briefing with the chief, Ellie would sit quietly or make an excuse to leave the room and not return. "Is there tree cover behind the houses that would provide a criminal ease of access? Could the bomb maker arrive at the homes unseen if he came in from the back?"

"It's a possibility. I haven't yet made a visit to the crime scenes," the chief told them. "I'm going to Solana tomorrow, if any of you could come along."

"I'll go," Angie said.

"I'd be happy to accompany you," Finch agreed.

Just then the youngest Roseland sister entered the sunroom still wearing her work apron. "What's cookin?"

Courtney was the same height as Angie, had the same color hair, and similar bright blue eyes. She was the family member who most loved their paranormal skills and helping the police investigate crimes. "Why didn't anyone tell me there was a meeting? What have I missed?"

"Have a seat," Angie said. "Chief Martin is telling us about something that's going on in Solana."

"The explosives?" With a slice of the tart on her plate, Courtney sat down, eager to hear the news.

Euclid jumped up to wedge himself in next to the young woman and she let him lick some of the custard from her finger.

The chief summarized the details he'd reported so far.

"What about the woman who picked up the bomb?" Courtney lifted a piece of the tart to her mouth.

"She'll survive although she'll require several surgeries to deal with the injuries to her hand and arm," Chief Martin said.

"At least she didn't lose a limb." Jenna tried to find something hopeful in the situation.

"Is there anyone in Solana who has some skill with pyrotechnics or fireworks or special effects?" Courtney asked. "Mr. Finch and I saw a crime show once where a guy used fireworks to set a fire at an apartment house."

"My friend hasn't reported being familiar with

anyone like that." The chief went to the side table to refresh his cup of coffee. "But that doesn't mean someone with those certain skills isn't living in Solana. The perpetrator might keep that information to himself."

"Are the victims of the bomber similar in any ways?" Finch asked. "Is the bomb maker targeting certain types of individuals?"

"The woman who was targeted is seventy-two-years old and has lived in her house for fifty years. The man who found the package in his mailbox is forty-seven and has lived in his house for five years." Chief Martin shrugged. "Different genders, different ages, different lengths of time in their homes."

"Okay," Courtney said. "Nothing similar there, but do they live in the same neighborhood?"

"They don't. They live six miles apart."

"So is it random?" Angie questioned. "Maybe the guy drives around looking for somewhere to leave a device. The street would have to be quiet and empty, nobody walking a dog or out for a jog. No roadwork going on. No mail truck, no school bus, no delivery services going by. He drives around looking for a house where no one will see him placing the device. The qualifying factor may be ease of opportunity, not who the potential victim is."

"That would make it harder to catch the criminal," Jenna suggested. "If it's random, no one will know where he might strike next."

Ellie's forehead creased in thought. "Do you think he'll strike again? Maybe he did what he wanted to do. Maybe he accomplished his goal. There might not be another incident."

"I think there will be," the chief said and as soon as he uttered the sentence, Euclid let out a loud howl causing Courtney to startle.

"Jeez, Euclid," she told the cat. "Give me some warning before you decide to screech like that."

The big orange boy flicked his enormous plume of a tail and scowled at her.

"Solana is a small town," the chief said. "Their police force is small as well. My friend, Benny Peterson, is worried things could get out of hand if the perp isn't found soon. Benny's afraid the criminal will become emboldened if he's able to allude law enforcement. He might escalate the planting of these incendiary devices. If that's what happens, then there will be fatalities. Luck can't hold out forever. This is what Benny hopes can be avoided."

"The person doing this may not be from Solana," Ellie pointed out. "He may drive in and leave as soon as he's planted a device. The culprit may be targeting the town for a specific reason."

"And if we can figure out the reason," Courtney said with excitement in her voice, "then it will make it easier to catch the creep."

Angie protectively placed her hand over her abdomen. Crimes, criminals, and bad things happening in the world had been having a stronger effect on her now that she was carrying a child. Jenna was also feeling impacted by negative events in the news, and she and Angie had talked many times about bringing children into what sometimes seemed a scary world.

"Our kids will be surrounded by people who love them," Jenna had said during their conversation.

"And we'll all work hard to help them become kind, respectful, considerate human beings," Angie added. *And we'll do everything in our power to keep them safe.*

3

When they stopped at the curb in front of a large ranch house, Jenna got out and helped Mr. Finch from the car. Angie and Chief Martin exited the police car and came to stand near the curb with Finch and Jenna.

"There aren't many trees on the sides or at the rear of the property," Finch observed. "Nothing for the perpetrator to hide in."

Jenna slipped on her sunglasses. "I noticed that, too. The neighborhood is pretty open. Not much cover for the guy when he placed the device."

Angie looked around the street. "But the perp put the bomb in the mailbox so he must have driven up close and slipped the bomb inside. What would that take? Ten seconds? Not even."

"So the criminal wouldn't need any cover to do what he did," Jenna said. "He was probably quick about it and was pulling away from the mailbox within seconds. Sometimes the post office uses private drivers in their own vehicles to deliver overnight packages. Having someone drive up and leave something in the mailbox wouldn't arouse suspicion if anyone saw it happen."

"Did anyone witness someone near the mailbox?" Angie asked. "Have the neighbors been questioned?"

"A lot of them have," Chief Martin told them. "But one guy refused to talk to us. He said he wasn't going to help us do our jobs."

"Nice guy," Angie grumped. "Hopefully he won't ever need police help with anything."

"Or any help from his neighbors." Finch tapped the ground with his cane.

A man came out of the ranch's front door and moved quickly down the walkway to speak with the foursome. He was in his forties, had dark brown hair, a few extra pounds, and looked like he worked out lifting weights. He greeted the chief and nodded to the others.

"Thanks for meeting us." The chief introduced Dennis Leeds to Finch and the sisters.

"The bomb was in the mailbox right here." Dennis gestured to the black box set on the mail post at the end of the driveway.

"What made you hesitant about it?" Angie asked.

Dennis ran his hand over his short brown hair. "I was working on some paperwork in my home office. I'm a plumber. I had the television on and a report came across about a bomb going off on a porch here in town. I was shocked by the news. Nothing happens in Solana. Later when I went to get the mail and saw a package in the box, I stopped before removing it. I don't really know why. I mean who would want to hurt *us*? We're normal people, we don't have enemies, we're not mixed up in anything weird."

"But you were uneasy about the package," Jenna said. "What did it look like? How big was it?"

Dennis used his hands to mimic the size and shape of the box. "It was about a foot long and eight inches wide. It was wrapped in brown paper. I knew I hadn't ordered anything and my wife doesn't like buying things online. She likes to see the product before she buys it. It seemed kind of big to have the post office deliver it. Why not use one of the parcel delivery services? All of those things raced through my mind in a couple of seconds. I closed the mailbox door and went back in the house."

"Did you call the police right away?" Mr. Finch asked.

"I stewed on it for a while," Dennis reported. "I was afraid to bother the police, especially because I knew they must be at the scene in town where the first bomb went off. I didn't want them to think I was some worrywart who had to get in on the excitement."

"But you called eventually?" Jenna questioned.

"My wife came home. I was in the living room and saw her car. It stopped at the mailbox. I ran to the front door and shouted to her not to take the mail out. When she came inside and I told her about the package, she took her phone out and placed a call to the police telling them there was something suspicious in the mailbox." Dennis shrugged. "I should have called them, but I felt like I was blowing it out of proportion. When Carol showed concern about it, it made me feel like I *wasn't* being unreasonable."

"As it turned out, you definitely weren't being too concerned for you and your wife's safety," Chief Martin said. "It was fortunate that you went with your instincts."

"Yeah." The hot sun caused some beads of perspiration to show on the man's forehead. "Would you like to come inside? Why don't we get out of the sun?"

The group went into the air-conditioned house and Dennis brought out some cans of seltzer and soda. "I should have bought some snacks and stuff."

"Not at all. The cold seltzer will hit the spot," Finch assured Dennis. "Thank you."

"Are you friendly with your neighbors?" Chief Martin asked.

"Sure. Most of them. We aren't best buddies or anything, but everyone's nice and we stop to talk when we see each other outside."

"Are there some neighbors who aren't so friendly?" Jenna questioned.

"The guy diagonally across from us. He's kind of odd. Stays to himself mostly. Seems like a grouch. He's only in his thirties, he's not some old coot or anything. I've barely said a few sentences to him."

"Is he new to the neighborhood?" Angie asked.

"He moved in about six months ago. The guy was shoveling the walkway one day and I stopped by to welcome him to the street. He gave me a weird look, said thanks, and went back inside the house. That was it. He didn't even finish the shoveling." Dennis shook his head recalling the neighbor's odd behavior.

"What is the man's name?" Finch asked.

"Dave Hanes. I wouldn't know it except I got some of his mail by mistake one day and I saw the name and address."

"Does Mr. Hanes live alone?" Jenna asked.

"He does. At least, I think so. Maybe there's another odd duck living inside who never comes out."

"Have you spoken with some of your other neighbors about the mail bomb?" Angie questioned.

"I have, yeah. They were all shocked. No one expects something like that to happen on your street, let alone in your own little town."

"Do you know the victim of the first bomb?" Angie set her can of seltzer on the coffee table.

"I don't. My wife doesn't know her either. We've never met the woman."

"Do you have any mutual acquaintances?"

A blank expression showed on Dennis's face as he considered the question. "I don't think so."

"Do you attend church?" Mr. Finch asked.

"No, we don't."

Chief Martin looked up from the small notebook

he was writing in. "Are you involved with any town committees or clubs?"

"I'm on the conservation commission. Most of our time is taken up by making sure any new building or renovation abides by the state wetlands laws. Sometimes I volunteer to help out at the local cable news network," Dennis said. "With running my business, I don't have much time do anything else."

"And what about your wife? Where does she work?" Jenna asked the man.

"She's a nurse at the hospital in Sweet Cove. She's been working there for about twenty years."

"Have either of you had any run-ins with anyone?" the chief asked.

"Run-ins? No. You mean like an argument or something?" Dennis blinked.

"A disagreement, a difficult client or patient, someone who seemed angry or annoyed with either of you."

"Just normal stuff. My wife often has difficult patients. She works in the emergency room. She sees a lot. She hasn't told me anything out of the ordinary."

"Did any of your neighbors notice someone near the mailbox the other day?" Angie asked.

"The woman next door saw the mail delivery person on the street that morning," Dennis said. "She was in her front yard and talked with him for a while."

Jenna got an idea. "Was it the same letter carrier who delivers the mail on this street every day?"

"Yeah, the same one as always. I asked about that. I wondered if someone new was doing the mail deliveries that day, but it was the same guy as always."

"No one noticed someone new in the neighborhood right before the bomb was found?" Jenna wondered if someone had been on the street checking the houses to see if there were people around.

"Nobody remembers seeing anyone suspicious."

"What about someone who didn't seem suspicious, but was new around here?" Chief Martin asked.

"There's a new nanny at the Boyd's house," Dennis said. "But why would a nanny have a reason to make and place bombs? It can't be her. She wouldn't have any place to build the devices."

"How long has the nanny been with the Boyds?" Angie asked.

"Maybe three months?" Dennis estimated.

"Were you at home all day on the day the bomb showed up in your mailbox?" Jenna drank from her can of seltzer.

Dennis shook his head. "I was working at a client's place in the morning. I went by the hardware store for some parts I needed for the next day, then I came home for lunch."

"Did you go out again after lunch?" Mr. Finch questioned.

"My afternoon client canceled so I decided to stay home and get caught up on paperwork."

"When did you go to the mailbox?" Angie tilted her head slightly in question.

"I worked until around 4pm. Then I decided to get the mail. I needed to stretch. I'd been hunched over doing the paperwork for too long."

"And when you went to the mailbox, you saw the package inside?"

"That's right. I'd just seen the news report about the woman who picked up a package from her porch and it exploded in her hand. I guess I'm superstitious. I saw the package in the mailbox and I got a little freaked out. I left everything in the box and went back inside the house."

"Was there anyone on the street or on the sidewalk when you were at your mailbox?" Angie asked the man.

"Just weird Dave Hanes. He was in his driveway. I didn't wave or anything."

"What was Mr. Hanes doing?"

"I didn't look over at him, but I saw him out of the corner of my eye." Dennis's expression clouded. "I could see he was watching me."

4

It was early evening with the sun lower in the sky as Angie stood near the grill next to her husband Josh, holding a platter for him to place the skewers of chicken and vegetables. The family had been eating dinner outside under the pergola whenever the weather was good which meant they'd been enjoying their meals in the open air for most of the summer.

The B and B guests were always invited to join the group for the evening meal, but tonight the visitors all had other plans. Courtney's boyfriend, Rufus, had a small bar set up where he could make drinks or pour wine, beer, seltzer, or soda into glasses and he was chatting away with Chief Martin and his wife, Lucille.

With Circe on his lap, Mr. Finch sat with his girl-friend, Betty, near the fire pit listening to her chatter on about the latest listings she'd acquired. Betty was a successful Sweet Cove Realtor who lived and breathed real estate and always had her finger on the pulse of what was going on in town and the surrounding areas.

"Orla and Mel want to sell their house."

One of Finch's eyebrows rode up. "They're not moving away, are they?"

"They want something different. They have too many stairs in their house. They want a master bedroom on the first floor so they don't have to manage steps as they age. I think they're being smart and proactive."

Courtney chuckled as she walked by the couple carrying a big bowl of salad. "I bet you'd agree with them if they wanted a four-story house with all the bedrooms on the upper floors," she teased the Real-tor. "You'd get to sell their current house and find them something new."

Betty flustered and defended herself. "I might not agree with a client's choices, but I'm smart enough to keep my opinions to myself ... most of the time. People have their own ideas and preferences. I only help them find what they want. In Orla's and

Mel's case, I happen to think they're being forward-thinking."

"I'm only joking with you. You're a good business person." Courtney smiled and went to the long wooden table to set down the salad bowl.

When the young woman had stepped away, Betty leaned close to Mr. Finch and winked at him. "She's wrong. I'm an *excellent* business person."

Finch patted Betty's hand in agreement.

Jack, a local lawyer and Ellie's boyfriend, held the back door open for her as she came outside carrying a serving dish of baked macaroni and cheese. The two whispered and flirted with one another as Jack took her free hand and helped her down the steps.

Jenna and her husband, Tom, were setting the table with plates, silverware, and water glasses. Euclid sat in one of the Adirondack chairs supervising the couple.

"Look at those two love birds." Courtney gestured to Jack and Ellie. "Why don't they get married already?"

"They're happy and in no rush." Tom wiped away a smudge on one of the goblets, and then with a sly grin, he asked, "What about you and your

Englishman lawyer? You've been dating for a long time now."

Courtney gave Tom an impish smile. "We're happy and in no rush," she said using her brother-in-law's own words.

"Nice come-back." Tom laughed. "Maybe lawyers are so analytical and logical they have to wait years before they can make such a big decision as marriage."

Courtney's eyes sparkled. "Maybe when the time is right, *I'll* be the one who proposes to Rufus."

"Don't doubt her," Jenna warned Tom.

"I would never doubt my youngest sister-in-law." Euclid trilled.

"That's a wise decision." Mr. Finch came over to the outside serving table to add some appetizers to his plate to share with Betty. "Miss Courtney is always full of surprises."

"I was just saying I might be the one who proposes to Rufus and not the other way around." Courtney placed light blue napkins next to each plate.

"It's a modern world and you are a modern young woman. Rufus would be a lucky man if you asked him to join you in marriage," Finch said nodding his head. "A lucky man indeed."

Courtney gave the older man a hug.

When all the food was ready, everyone took seats under the pergola that was wrapped with glimmering, tiny, white lights. When Tom lit the tiki torches standing around the periphery of the yard, they gave off a warm, golden glow.

"Thankfully, there haven't been any more pipe bomb incidents," Tom said as he held a platter so Jenna could scoop some potato salad onto the plate.

The chief gave a grateful nod. "I hope the perp isn't quietly biding his time before he strikes again."

"Any leads?" Betty asked.

The chief said, "We're still doing interviews, talking to the neighbors and to anyone who was walking or driving past the houses on the day the bombs were left. So far, no clues and no suspects."

"No one saw anything suspicious?" Betty asked.

"Not so far." Chief Martin added with a positive tone in his voice. "It's early yet. These things take time."

Lucille, a professor of psychology at the nearby university, shook her head as she raised her wine glass. "No matter how many years Phillip works in law enforcement and I do research in my field, understanding the criminal mind never gets easier."

"Maybe because of all the publicity, the guy is

afraid to do anything more and has given up," Jack suggested.

"It's possible," Lucille said, "but the more likely scenario is that the criminal is excited by all the attention he's getting which fuels him to want to plant more bombs. My thinking is he's biding his time, letting things cool down a little, then he'll strike again when people think it's over."

"Do you think this criminal lives in Solana?" Rufus passed the bottle of wine to Tom.

"That's hard to say," Lucille told them. "He may have a grudge against the town for some perceived slight. He may hold grudges against the two people he targeted. Or he might not have any connection to the town or its inhabitants and is on a spree for the heck of it. He could be inspired by something he read about another person planting bombs. Without more information, it's difficult to make a reasonable supposition."

"What a mess," Tom groaned. "How can you ever catch someone like this?"

"It's not easy." The chief let a sigh escape from his throat. "The guy makes a mistake, a passerby gets a look at him or his vehicle, a victim sees him delivering the device. Bits of information, little things we gather, some lucky breaks can all add up. We do the work and hope we find something that leads us to the perpetrator."

"Before it happens again," Betty said.

When the meal was over, Lucille, Betty, Rufus, and Jack cleared the table and took the dirty dishes into the house where they put the tea kettle on the stove and made coffee.

Chief Martin said, "Agnes Shield, the woman who was injured by one of the bombs is now well enough to be questioned. Another officer and I spoke with her this morning, but I'd like a couple of you to come with me to see her again. She was heavily medicated today. The doctor told me to return tomorrow afternoon and I might have better luck."

"I can go," Courtney looked over at Mr. Finch. "I have the afternoon off from the candy store. Unless you want to go, Mr. Finch and I'll stay at the shop."

"I think you should go this time. You're very kind with older people. You might have a rapport with Mrs. Shield."

"I have quite a few orders to get out tomorrow," Jenna said. "I'll go the next time."

"I can go tomorrow," Angie said. "Louisa and the new employees can handle the museum bake shop in the afternoon."

Josh took his wife's hand. "Do you feel up to helping on this investigation? You've just gotten over the morning sickness. You don't want to get rundown. Ellie, Courtney, and Mr. Finch can help the chief."

Ellie's eyes widened and she opened her mouth to speak, but decided not to protest. Criminal cases took an emotional toll an Ellie and were something she preferred to avoid, but if she had to stand-in for Jenna and Angie, she would do it ... despite wishing she could help in any other way possible besides getting involved with a case.

"I'm fine now." Angie dabbed at her lips with her napkin. "And anyway, I can't let everyone else have all the fun. If I start to get tired or I don't feel well, I'll step aside and the rest of the family can take up the slack."

A look of relief spread over Ellie's face. "You know I'll do it, if you and Jenna can't."

Courtney chuckled. "Ellie's unspoken next sentence is, *but please don't make me*."

Ellie gave her younger sister a scowl as the others laughed knowing very well that Courtney was right.

Jenna's facial expression turned serious. "Has Mrs. Shield lost her hand?"

Chief Martin said, "The surgeons were able to

save most of the hand. She lost the ring finger and the pinky on her left hand."

"The poor woman," Ellie's voice shook at the thought of someone losing part of their hand.

"At least, she didn't lose the hand completely," Tom said. "She'll be able to manage just fine with the two fingers missing."

"She'll be having extensive rehab," the chief told the group, "many hours of physical and occupational therapy. The outlook is positive that Mrs. Shield will be able to return to her normal life and routine."

"Let's hope," Angie said, "that there aren't any more victims who have to endure what Mrs. Shield is going through with her hand."

"Or worse," Courtney frowned.

5

Agnes Shield rested in her hospital bed with her eyes closed, her white pouf of hair spread out on the pillow. An IV's tube led to the woman's inner forearm and her left hand was wrapped in white gauze and bandages giving no hint that two of the woman's fingers were missing.

Chief Martin spoke her name softly and Mrs. Shield's eyes fluttered open. When she saw the chief, Agnes pushed herself into a slightly upright position.

"Hello. You were here yesterday."

The voice was stronger than Angie was expecting.

"Yes, I was, but you were too tired to talk." The

chief approached the bed. "Are you able to answer some questions today? Are you feeling up to it?"

"I can talk with you." Mrs. Shield let her bandaged hand rest in her lap as she shifted to look at the two young women.

Chief Martin introduced Angie and Courtney as police consultants and then he took three folding metal chairs from their position against the wall and set them near the bed so they could sit.

"How are you doing, Mrs. Shield?" Angie asked with a gentle tone.

"I'm doing okay actually." The older woman ran her hand over her puffy white hair. "I must look a fright."

"You look fine," Chief Martin assured her. "You've been through quite a lot."

Mrs. Shield drew in a long breath. "At least, he didn't kill me." She glanced down at her hand. "I can deal with this."

"Can you tell us about the day? How it happened, what you were doing?" the chief requested.

The woman let her head rest back against the pillow. "It was a normal day. I'd been to the market in the morning. I walked two miles. I do that every day, rain or shine. There were some housekeeping tasks to get done and then I had my lunch. My husband is away with a friend of his for a few days. They enjoy camping. I don't like it at all so I don't go along. After lunch, I worked in the backyard on the flower garden, then I took a shower and sat down to read for a while."

Angie, Courtney, and Chief Martin sat quietly waiting for Mrs. Shield to go on, and right before the chief was going to ask a question to get her talking again, she spoke.

"I dozed in my chair holding my novel. I woke thinking I'd heard a noise on the porch. I went to the window to look out, but I didn't see anyone there. I was about to return to my chair when I noticed a package near the front door so I went out to see what it was."

Mrs. Shield bit her lower lip for a second and went on with her story. "I bent to pick it up. I remember wondering what it was because I hadn't ordered anything. All I recall from that moment was a blinding flash of light. There must have been a sound, but I don't remember hearing anything. The next thing I knew I was here in the hospital." The woman shook her head slowly.

"When you went out to the porch," Chief Martin

asked, "did you notice anyone on the sidewalk or getting into a car?"

"I don't believe I saw anyone. Some things, I just don't remember though. The doctor told me it's not unusual for memories to come back over time."

"You said a noise woke you," Angie said. "Was it the noise of a car engine? Or do you think it was more the sound of feet on the porch?"

Mrs. Shield put her hand against the side of her face. "I'm not sure what it was. I only know some-thing caused me to stir from my nap."

"Was the living room window open?" Courtney asked, her blue eyes looking closely at the woman's face.

"Yes, it was. The day was warm, but not sticky or humid. I like to keep the windows open in the summer. The winter can be long, and I miss hearing the birds and having a bit of a breeze coming into the house."

"Are you retired?" the chief asked.

"No, I work part time at the hospital. I'm a psychi-atric nurse practitioner. I worked full time until I was sixty-seven and then I asked about working three days a week. The administration allowed it. I enjoy my job."

Angie's mind was racing over the possibilities

that a patient of Mrs. Shield's may have carried out the crime. "Is it a difficult job?"

"It can be, but most of the time things go smoothly. I like helping people manage their conditions." Mrs. Shield yawned.

"Can you go along with our questions for a little bit longer?" the chief asked. "Or shall we end our visit and return another day?"

"I'm okay to continue. I want to help you catch this person."

"Please let us know if you've had enough for the day." The chief had a notebook on his knee and a pen in his hand. "Have you worked at the hospital for a long time?"

"I started as a registered nurse and worked for about ten years before deciding to return to school for my master's degree. When I finished the advanced study, I was hired at the hospital. That was about twenty-five years ago so all in all, I've worked there for about thirty-five years ... and still going strong. I like the three day a week schedule. It gives me time to do other things."

"Do you have any hobbies?" Courtney asked the woman.

"I quilt, I garden, I like to exercise by walking

daily. I read quite a lot. I take care of my four-year-old granddaughter one day a week."

Angie sat up. "Where do you care for her? At your house or hers?"

"I go to my daughter's house. Ava's things are there. It's easier."

"Where does your daughter live?" Angie asked.

"In Silver Cove." Mrs. Shield tried to stifle another yawn.

"Have any of your patients been difficult lately?" the chief inquired. "Was there a run-in or an altercation of any kind?"

"No, nothing."

"Did anyone threaten you?"

"What? Good grief, no."

"What about a patient who was angry or upset or threatening in some way? Maybe not to you, but in general or to someone in particular?"

"There are always patients who are angry and upset. It's the nature of the field. My job is to provide mental health care to those dealing with behavioral issues or mental health disorders."

"No one stands out to you? You can't think of a patient who might have the desire to hurt you?" the chief questioned.

46

Mrs. Shield's eyes went wide. "Hurt me? Gosh, I can't think of anyone."

"How about a colleague or someone else you work with or come in contact with at the hospital. Have you had words with someone or some difficulty with anyone in the workplace?"

Mrs. Shield shook her head. "No one. There are always petty annoyances when people work together, but nothing blows up into anything. Everyone works to keep friendly or polite relationships with each other."

"How about in other places?" Angie asked. "Are you a member of any town boards? Do you do volunteer work anywhere? Any community type of activities that you're involved in?"

"I'm involved with the garden club and I deliver meals to the elderly once a week."

"You're a very busy person," Courtney smiled.

Mrs. Shield frowned. "I hope my injury doesn't slow me down. I enjoy my routines and interactions. I'd like to continue with them."

"I don't see why you wouldn't be able to keep doing the things you enjoy," Angie said. "Your rehab therapy will help you with any compensatory strategies you might need to adopt. I'd bet you'll be able to return to doing anything you want to do."

"You have a very full and active life." Courtney nodded and then asked a question that had been picking at her. "Have you noticed anyone hanging around the neighborhood recently? Maybe someone lingering a little too long or maybe someone giving the area a lot of scrutiny?"

"Well, three days a week I'm not home until 3:30pm and one day I'm in Silver Cove with my granddaughter. I'm not at home much during the day so I can't say if anyone suspicious is lurking around or not."

"Can you think of anyone who might have a grudge against you?" the chief asked. "Has anyone you've known ever seemed to blow some small disagreement with you out of proportion? Maybe not anything recent?"

Mrs. Shield lay quietly for a while as she thought about the questions the chief posed to her. "Really, nothing comes to mind, certainly nothing that would cause someone to try to kill me. No, it must have been random. The front porch was a good place to leave the object. Someone coming home or going out would see it easily. Maybe the neighborhood was empty at the time the person left the bomb. There aren't many people around when it's warm out during the day. People are working, kids are at camp. If it's hot, people stay inside where it's air conditioned. Someone could easily drop something in a front yard or at the front of a house without anyone in the neighborhood seeing them do it. Unfortunately for me. I overheard some nurses say someone in town had a suspicious package in their mailbox. Is that true?"

"It's true," Chief Martin said. "The man heard about your accident on the news and when he spotted the package in his mailbox, he left it alone and called the police."

"Well," Mrs. Shield said. "Maybe some good came from what happened to me. If the man didn't know about the bomb on my porch, he may have removed the package from his mailbox and been killed by it. Perhaps, my *accident* saved his life."

6

When the bake shop closed at 3pm, Angie and Orla cleaned up the tables and floor, prepped some muffins for the next day, washed out the coffee machines, and put dishes and cups away in the cabinets.

Jenna and Mr. Finch sat on stools at the counter sipping coffee and chatting. Jenna had worked in her shop creating new jewelry pieces while waiting on customers who came into the small store at the back of the Victorian. Finch had spent the day in the candy store making fudge, tiny tarts, and several flavors of chocolates and on his way home, he decided to stop in to Angie's bake shop for a coffee and a pastry.

"Are you enjoying working here?" Finch asked Orla.

"I love it." Orla was cleaning out the pastry case. "I love seeing the townspeople and the tourists and since I'm an early riser, the hours are perfect for me." The woman smiled and nodded to Angie. "And the boss isn't bad either."

"Betty Hayes told us you and Mel are thinking of selling your house." Jenna picked at a blueberry muffin.

Orla sighed. "We didn't want to sell it so soon, but it's just not the right fit for us. Mel has a bad knee and the stairs make it worse. We'd like a bedroom and bathroom on the first floor. We contacted Betty and as soon as we have a few of the rooms freshly painted, it will go on the market."

"You plan to stay in Sweet Cove?" Finch asked.

"Oh, my, yes. We love this town."

Talk moved to the coming babies and how Angie and Jenna were feeling.

"February will be a busy month for the Rose-lands," Orla smiled. "I can't wait to see these two cherubs. Will you be putting them in daycare while you're working?"

Jenna set her coffee mug down. "We were

thinking of hiring a nanny. Someone who would be able to take care of both of the babies."

Angie smiled at Mr. Finch. "We have someone who is interested, but he runs a store in town and can only help out part-time."

Orla's eyes widened. "Victor? How wonderful. You couldn't ask for a kinder, more loving person."

Finch blushed. "It would be the joy of my life to care for these two precious wonders."

Orla put her hand over her heart. "How touching."

"The only problem is that it's hard to find someone who will work part-time on the days Mr. Finch is at the candy store," Angie said. "Most nannies want a fulltime position."

"I only work part-time here at the bake shop," Orla said. "I'd be happy to care for the children on the days Victor is working in his store."

Angie and Jenna stared at Orla.

"You would?" Jenna asked, disbelieving. "Really?"

Orla had a wide smile on her face. "Would the children be here at the Victorian?"

Angie nodded. "We thought that would be the best thing since I'll be working in this store most of the time and Jenna has her jewelry store and work-shop here."

"I'd love to do it. Of course, if you want to hire a professional, I understand."

"You've had kids of your own. You and Mel are our dear friends. We'd be thrilled if you wanted to share the load with Mr. Finch," Angie said.

Orla turned her hazel eyes to Finch. "I think we'd make a good team."

"I agree, Ms. Orla."

"We can watch for and encourage any skills the children demonstrate, too," Orla said.

"You think they'll have skills?" Jenna questioned.

"If they're both girls, I'd bet money on it." Orla nodded. "Your grandmother's line of women with paranormal powers runs long and deep. I don't believe the *skills* have ever skipped a generation, as far back as we know." Orla had powers of her own and had spent decades traveling the world working with those who had abilities. She never discussed much about her talents or her duties, but the Rose-lands and Mr. Finch knew she was a powerful force for good within the paranormal community. "I believe Victor and I would be very helpful to the children."

Mr. Finch had skills as well. He could pick up on

feelings and sensations floating on the air, and sometimes, by shaking someone's hand or touching them, he was able to read their intentions.

Orla said, "Mel and I will have to find a house close by so it will be easy for me to get to the Victorian. I'll have to speak to Betty about what might be available in the neighborhood."

"You know," Mr. Finch said, "I've been thinking of selling my house."

Everyone turned to the man with wide eyes.

"What? Why? Where would you go?" Angie's voice held a slight tone of panic.

"Are you moving in with Betty?" Jenna asked.

"Oh, my, no, Miss Jenna. We're not married, and as much as we love each other, we've both been living alone for so long I'm not sure it would be wise to share a home together." Finch's eyes sparkled as he gave the women a wink. "And besides, for us, I think time apart makes our spark glow stronger."

Jenna, Angie, and Orla chuckled.

"Whatever works for you," Jenna told the man.

"But why do you want to leave your house?" Angie asked.

"It's too big for me. I'm one person. I don't need so many rooms. I'd prefer something smaller and cozier."

"Have you started looking around?" Angie didn't like the idea of Mr. Finch being further away from them and told him so.

Finch smoothed his mustache. "Well, I have an idea, but I've not yet brought it up with any of you."

"What is it?" Angie felt slightly worried.

"Would it be possible for me to rent one of the carriage house apartments? On a long term basis?"

Angie's heart skipped a beat. "The carriage house ... you want to move into the carriage house?"

"If it wouldn't inconvenience anyone." Finch looked from Jenna to Angie. "As long as there aren't future plans for the apartments."

"Of course you can live in one of the apartments." Angie smiled with relief that Finch would still be living close to them. "That would be perfect."

"You'd only be steps from the Victorian," Jenna said. "It would be wonderful."

"I'll speak to Miss Ellie about it to be sure it wouldn't interfere with her bed and breakfast business. Some of the guests like having an apartment when they stay here."

Angie waved her hand in the air. "There are two apartments available. A guest can have the other one if they want an apartment. Tom says there's plenty of room to build another apartment off the back of the carriage house. Would you rather a first floor living space? We can talk about building you a new place."

"I never thought of that," Finch said with interest in the idea.

Jenna smiled. "I'll talk to Tom about it later tonight."

Orla said, "If you're going to sell your house, Victor, maybe Mel and I would be interested in purchasing it from you. Do you have a bedroom on the first floor?"

"There is a good-sized den on the first floor that would be perfect for a bedroom. There's also a full bathroom."

Orla clasped her hands together. "I'd be so close to the Victorian."

Finch beamed. "There's a brick walkway from my house through the small grove of trees to the rear of the Victorian. I had it put in to make it easier for me to pass from my home to this one."

"Everything's falling into place." Jenna's face was bright. "You'll each have homes that are more suited to your needs, and our babies now have their nannies."

Ellie stepped into the bake shop through the door that led into the mansion's kitchen to see the four people hugging one another. "What have I missed?"

Each of them took turns explaining the reasons why they were happy.

"That's great news," Ellie said. "It will be wonderful to have you even closer to us, Mr. Finch, and it will be so convenient for Orla and Mel to be nearby. The babies are very lucky to have so many loving people in their lives."

Jenna said, "And Orla and Mr. Finch will help the kids develop their skills."

"Oh." Ellie's face dropped. "I didn't think about that. I didn't realize the babies would be born with their own abilities."

"We're guessing they will," Angie pointed out. "We don't know for sure."

"Paranormal skills run deep in your genes," Orla told Ellie. "It's very likely these new members of the family will have them as well."

Ellie looked uneasy. "How early do things like that show up?"

Orla slipped the washed and dried pastry racks into place in the glass cases. "It can happen around the time they begin to walk, or the skills can take their time and show up later in life, but most skills make an appearance by adolescence." The older woman picked up on Ellie's discomfort. "Not to worry. Things develop slowly. Children show signs of their abilities, but they need guidance to understand what they can do and it takes years for them to come into their own."

"They won't do anything *unusual* in front of strangers?" Ellie questioned.

"Not at all. They'll learn to control themselves before their skills strengthen."

"That's a relief." Ellie's posture became more relaxed, and then she looked over at Angie. "Oh. I forgot. Chief Martin is trying to get in touch with you. He said you're not answering his texts or calls."

"I forgot to turn my phone back on. I wonder what he wants." Hurrying to get her phone, a cold shiver of worry washed over Angie's skin.

7

Chief Martin wanted Angie and one of her sisters or Mr. Finch to accompany him to see Agnes Shield's neighbor. The woman called him and ranted about safety and the bomb and what were the police going to do about it. The chief tried to calm her over the phone by explaining how law enforcement would proceed with the case, until she told him she saw something on the day Agnes was injured.

Emily Lancer was in her late seventies, was short and round, had light blue eyes and white hair cut in short layers around her face. She was waiting on the porch for the chief, Angie, and Jenna and stood when she saw them pull into the driveway. A few minutes later, Chief Martin's friend, Chief Benny

Peterson of Solana, pulled up to the house. Peterson was in his late fifties, slim, medium height, and graying.

After introductions, they all went inside to Mrs. Lancer's air-conditioned sitting room. The home was neat and lovingly decorated with velvet sofas, cherry side tables, a coffee table, and a heavy Persian rug of soft, muted colors.

"Please sit down," Mrs. Lancer gestured to the chairs and sofas. "We have carafes of iced tea and lemonade, and there are cookies on the table. Please help yourselves."

Chief Martin had his notebook on his knee as he balanced a small plate with two cookies on his lap. "Thank you for seeing us. Have you spoken with Mrs. Shield since the accident?"

"It wasn't an accident," Mrs. Lancer corrected. "It was a deliberate act to kill or maim someone. And no, I haven't spoken with Agnes. We sent her flowers and I have plans to go visit her tomorrow."

"We saw her today. She's doing well. I'm sure she'll be happy to see you," the chief said.

"I'm glad to hear it." Mrs. Lancer shuddered. "I can't stop thinking about what happened. It could have been me or my husband. For some reason, the attacker chose Agnes's house to leave the bomb. It could have been our front porch. Who knows why? Luck or not, that's what it adds up to."

"You were at home when the bomb went off?" Chief Peterson asked.

"I was." Mrs. Lancer wrapped her arms around herself. "What a sound, like the whole town was going up in a blast."

"Can you tell us where you were?" Chief Martin asked.

"I was in my kitchen. I was making a late lunch. The windows shook when the bomb blasted. I was afraid a plane had crashed nearby or we were having an earthquake or some such thing. I ran to the front porch to see what was going on. I didn't notice at first, but part of Agnes's porch had been destroyed. Part of the railings and the slats of the porch were gone. I couldn't fathom what had happened."

The woman appeared visibly shaken from reliving the event.

"What did you do next?" Jenna asked.

"When I saw the porch rails blown apart, I called to Agnes."

"Did you stay on your porch when you called to her?" Jenna asked the next question.

"Yes, I did. I must have been in shock or something because I didn't think to move," Mrs. Lancer said. "I heard a moan coming from Agnes's porch. I managed to get moving and hurried over to see what happened. There she was, lying on the floor. I saw the blood. I looked all around trying to see if anyone was outside. I didn't know if she'd been shot or what. I felt panicky. Was someone outside with a rifle picking people off? I ran into my house and called the police."

"Did you stay inside?" Angie questioned.

"I did. I was afraid to go back out." Mrs. Lancer pushed at the side of her hair with shaking fingers. "I'm a coward, I guess. I left Agnes alone out there."

"You did the right thing," Angie told the woman. "There could have been a gunman. You were right to stay indoors."

"What happened when the police arrived?" Chief Peterson asked.

"I looked out of the front door. I stepped onto the porch. I told them I was the one who called. I told them Agnes was hurt." Mrs. Lancer put her hand on her stomach. "It makes me ill to talk about it."

"Would you like to take a break?" Chief Martin asked.

"I'm okay." The woman's cheeks were bright pink.

"Was your husband at home when the incident happened?" Angie questioned.

Mrs. Lancer shook her head. "He was out shopping for a new car. He didn't get home until dinner time. He doesn't listen to the radio when he's driving so he had no idea there was a bomb or that Agnes had been hurt."

"Did the police tell you a bomb had gone off?"

"Not in so many words. They asked me what I heard. They asked me if I heard Agnes speaking to anyone. They told me to keep the doors locked and not to handle any suspicious or unexpected packages. If I saw one, I should go inside and immediately call the police. From their questions, and from what I heard and what I saw, I was certain a bomb package must have blown up on Agnes's porch."

"When we spoke on the phone," Chief Martin said, "you told me you saw something."

Mrs. Lancer squeezed her lips together for a moment and then said, "I saw a delivery man. I saw him walking down Agnes's walkway to the street."

Angie's heart pounded. "What time was this?"

"I don't know. I didn't bother to check the time. I was in the kitchen and when I turned around, I caught sight of the man walking away." Mrs. Lancer gestured towards the window and then to the back of the house. "The kitchen is open to the family room and the windows look out over the side yard. I saw the man walking away from Agnes's porch."

"What did he look like?" Jenna leaned forward. "Can you describe him for us?"

"Like a normal man. He had on sunglasses. He had on dark slacks and a white short-sleeved shirt. It was like a Polo shirt. I thought it looked like a uniform."

"Was he tall? Short?"

"Medium," Mrs. Lancer said.

"What color was his hair?" Chief Peterson asked.

"He had on a cap, you know, like a baseball hat."

"Did he have any facial hair? A mustache? A beard?"

"I don't think so."

"How old did the man seem?" Angie asked the woman.

Mrs. Lancer tapped her cheek with her index finger as she thought over the question. "Not an older man. He moved quick like he was younger, but not a teenager."

Chief Peterson asked, "Did you see his delivery truck?"

"I would have had to come in here to see the street so, no, I didn't see a truck. There wasn't anything unusual about a delivery man being in the neighborhood. I didn't see any need to look out at him."

"Did you recognize what he was wearing? Did it make you think of a certain delivery service or company?" Angie asked.

"I thought about that and I don't know the answer." Mrs. Lancer clutched her hands together. "It wasn't a uniform used by the usual delivery companies. He didn't look like them. He didn't look like a postal worker either. I guess I assumed he was a delivery person for a national company, but the more I think about it, the more I realize he could have been pretending to be affiliated with a known business."

Jenna tried to jog the woman's memory. "Was there a name or a logo or anything like that on the man's shirt?"

Mrs. Lancer lifted one shoulder in a shrug. "I didn't notice."

"After you saw the delivery man leaving, did the bomb go off right away?" Chief Martin asked the woman.

"No. Maybe thirty minutes after I saw the man. Agnes must have come out to get the mail and spotted the package."

"Would you recognize this man if you saw him again?"

Mrs. Lancer shook her head sadly. "I don't see how I could. He wore sunglasses, had on the hat. I didn't see much of his face. He walked by briskly. I only had my eyes on him for a couple of seconds. I'm sorry."

"It's fine," Chief Martin encouraged the woman. "It gives us information we didn't have before. Every little bit helps. It will all add up. We need every piece of information to put it all together."

Mrs. Lancer seemed to brighten a little after the chief spoke.

"Were you and Agnes friends?" Chief Peterson asked.

"We were friendly. Agnes and I, and our husbands would have dinner together on occasion. Maybe once every two months. Agnes is still working, her husband, too. She's a smart woman."

"Did Agnes tell you anything about an argument or a run-in with anyone?" Chief Peterson asked.

Mrs. Lancer sat up straight with wide eyes. "She had a run-in with someone?"

"We don't know. We're trying to find out if she'd run into someone who might have argued with her or caused trouble of some kind. A patient, a colleague, an acquaintance?"

"I don't know. Agnes didn't mention anything like that to me." Mrs. Lancer wrung her hands absent-mindedly. "Did the delivery man leave the package on Agnes's porch because some killer sent it to her or was he a fake delivery man who targeted Agnes himself? Did he want to hurt Agnes or did he just look for a house where it was easy to drop off a package?"

"We don't know yet," Chief Peterson said.

"Was he looking for any random house to drop the bomb at? He couldn't have been out to get Agnes specifically. There's no possible reason he would want to hurt her ... she's a very nice person who gets along with everyone. It had to be random."

8

It was late afternoon when Angie, Courtney, and Jenna took a stroll to Main Street to browse in the stores and take a break from their busy lives. Sweet Cove's main street extended from the north end of town near the large common and park down to the southern tip where another popular tourist area known as Coveside was located. Coveside bordered the picturesque harbor and consisted of restaurants, small shops, and brick sidewalks. The central street near the Victorian also had popular shops, quaint pubs, cafes and restaurants, and flowers spilling over from window boxes and pots set near the entrances to the establishments.

The temperature was milder than it had been

and the air carried very little humidity making it a perfect afternoon to stroll through town.

"I'm caught up on my jewelry shipping thanks to you and Courtney and Ellie helping out," Jenna said. "There might be another huge shipment day coming up so I might press you all into service again soon."

Courtney chuckled. "That's fine. As usual, we'll send you a bill for our services."

Jenna smiled. "And I'll throw it in the trash as usual."

As they passed a new shop, Courtney stopped to look in the window. "Hey, look at this. They carry baby clothes and supplies. Let's go in."

The three young women stepped inside to the cozy, beautifully decorated, softly-lit store brimming with racks of baby and children's clothes, cribs and hand-painted furniture, strollers, and toys.

"This stuff is beautiful." Courtney admired a small, white dresser with animals and balloons painted on it.

Jenna held up a few onesies for Angie to see. "Look how tiny these are."

Angie ran her hand over a soft, light pink blanket. "We'll have to start thinking about preparing our nurseries pretty soon."

With a beaming smile, Jenna looked at her twin

sister. "It will be like our kids are twins, they'll be born so close together."

"I'm glad they're going to have each other to play with and go to school together." Angie gave her sister's arm an affectionate squeeze.

The three young women left the baby store and strolled to their friend, Francine's, stained glass shop where they were greeted warmly.

"What a nice surprise." Francine's green eyes were like emeralds. Slim and petite with blond hair, the woman had a warm, friendly, and vivacious personality.

Francine had a workshop and a small store attached to her house in Silver Cove, but decided to expand to the center of Sweet Cove for the foot traffic and tourist business. She'd hired Mel Abel to assist in the stores and was teaching him how to create the stained-glass designs so he could help with production.

"How is the museum bake shop working out?" Francine asked.

"It's even better than expected," Angie told her. "Business is booming. I've had to hire more help."

"Congratulations. You could open a shop on a deserted island and it would be a hit," Francine kidded.

The sisters admired a gorgeous stained-glass lamp made in the Tiffany-style and they praised Francine for her design and skill at creating such functional and beautiful objects.

"Have you heard about the trouble down in Solana? It's the talk of the town, the whole area, really. Pipe bombs being left at people's homes? It's so terrible. I'm acquainted with one of the victims, Agnes Shield."

"You know her?" Jenna asked.

"Her daughter lives in Silver Cove on my street. She's only a few houses away from me. I see Agnes outside with her grandchild. She's a nice woman, seems smart. She's still working as a nurse practitioner. I sent her some flowers. I hope she'll be able to keep active."

"We met her at the hospital." Angie explained they'd gone with Chief Martin to take notes as he interviewed the injured woman. Francine knew that the sisters did some research for the police when they needed help.

"How was she? Will she be okay?"

"The doctor told us Agnes would make a full recovery and would receive therapy to accommodate the loss of her fingers."

"That's wonderful," Francine smiled. "Is she able

to receive visitors? I'd love to drop in to see her."

"I think so," Jenna said. "Why not call the hospital to be sure."

"Do the police have any suspects?"

The sisters weren't free to discuss such things so Angie told their friend that they didn't have that sort of information.

Francine nodded in understanding. "That guy in Solana who received the bomb in his mailbox was lucky he didn't touch the thing and called the police instead. I don't know if I'd have the presence of mind to do that. I think I'd just grab the package along with the mail without thinking."

"I guess the perpetrator is hoping that's what people will do." Courtney frowned at the thought.

"Are the police thinking its random or targeted?" Francine questioned as she dusted some of the lamps and jewelry boxes on the shelves.

"They don't know yet." Angie looked at some stained-glass suncatchers hanging in the window.

Francine offered her opinion. "I think its random. Why would someone target Agnes Shield? She's a pleasant, caring person, easy to talk with, has a calm personality. I can't picture her arguing with anyone. She'd go out of her way to be accommodating. The man who received the pipe bomb doesn't live close to Agnes. They're different ages, different genders, they don't work in the same field or at the same place. Maybe the news reports left out some things that might connect the two people."

Angie had seen some of the police reports and there didn't seem to be a link of any kind between Agnes Shield and Dennis Leeds except for the fact they lived in the same town.

"They both live in Solana," Courtney pointed out. "Maybe some nut has a grudge against the town."

"So you think it's someone who lives in Solana, or did live there once?" Francine asked.

"It's a possibility, but everything is a possibility at this point."

"The police are going to need a big break in this case," Jenna said. "The guy is going to have to make a mistake or someone is going to have to see something."

"Do you know Agnes Shield's husband?" Angie asked her friend.

"I don't. Why do you ask?"

"I wondered what sort of person he was and if they have a strong marriage."

Francine's eyes widened. "You don't think her husband is behind these package bombs?"

"I'm suspicious of most people." Angie was only half-kidding. She'd seen quite a bit while helping the police and realized that truth could be stranger than fiction. "The husband might want to get rid of Agnes so he put the bomb on their porch and then placed a bomb in the other man's mailbox to throw the investigators off."

"Gosh." Francine looked horrified.

"I didn't consider that the bombs might have been placed by a family member," Jenna said.

"I should have thought of that," Courtney said. "Mr. Finch and I watch so many crime shows where the criminal is someone the victim knows. It would be clever to leave bombs at other homes to hide the fact that Agnes was the real victim. Does Agnes get along with her daughter?"

"She seems to," Francine said. "Oh, no. You don't think the daughter could be the bomber?"

"Does Agnes have any other kids?" Jenna questioned.

"I don't know. I think she only has the one daughter."

"What's her name?" Angie asked.

"Jen Bishop. She's always been friendly whenever I see her. She doesn't seem angry or resentful. She seems grateful to have her mother's help."

"Do you know where the daughter works?"

"She's a chemical engineer. She works in Peabody at a research facility."

"Chemical engineer, huh?" Courtney's face took on an expression of suspicion. "Would someone like that know how to make a bomb?"

"You could probably learn how to make one from the internet," Angie suggested.

"But a chemical engineer might have an advantage in understanding devices like the ones left in Solana," Jenna said.

"I can't see it," Francine said firmly. "Jen Bishop would be the last person I would suspect of such a thing. Trying to kill her own mother? Never."

"What about her husband?" Courtney asked. "What does he do?"

"I'm not sure. It has something to do with engineering, but I don't know what sort."

"Does Mr. Bishop get along with his mother-in-law?" Courtney wondered if there might be bad blood between them.

"I don't know," Francine said. "I assume so. Agnes never speaks ill of him. I don't recall her ever saying anything negative about him."

"Did Agnes ever mention a falling out with anyone?" Angie asked.

Francine shook her head. "No. Not to me. I don't see her that often, just when we cross paths outside."

"Does she seem to enjoy her job?"

"Yes, definitely. She reduced her workload to three days a week so she would have time to help with her grandchild. Agnes told me it was the perfect schedule for her."

Something about the conversation pulled at Angie. There was something discussed that made her feel anxious, but the reason for it was unclear. She made a mental note to ask Chief Martin about Agnes's husband, her daughter, and son-in-law.

"Maybe the bomber has stopped," Francine offered. "Maybe he got scared off by the media attention. He's probably frightened to try it again."

"He may be lying low for a while," Courtney said, "but I bet he won't stop."

"If he *was* trying to kill Agnes or Dennis Leeds and was using the other person to throw off the police, will he try again to kill his intended target?" Angie asked. "Could Agnes or Mr. Leeds still be in danger?"

9

Angie, Jenna, and Courtney walked along Main Street after leaving Francine's shop when a police cruiser pulled over to the curb and jolted to a stop. The passenger side window went down and Chief Martin leaned over from the driver's seat.

"There's been another incident. Can you come along?"

The sisters got into the car and the chief sped down the street with his light flashing.

"What's happened?" Angie sat in the front seat.

"Another bomb. A mother and her teenaged daughter decided to spend the afternoon watching a movie. Since the air is cooler today, they thought it would be pleasant to have a fire in the fireplace."

Courtney said, "I'm going out on a limb here and will guess the fire in the fireplace wasn't so pleasant after all?"

"It blew up. Not the fireplace itself, but one of the logs had been hollowed out and a bomb was put inside. When the fire started, it went off."

Jenna groaned. "Are the mother and daughter...?"

"Alive, but badly injured. They were rushed to the hospital." The chief took a quick glance at Angie. "Do you think it would be possible for Mr. Finch to meet us at the house in Solana?"

"I can ask him." Angie took out her phone and texted Mr. Finch the address. In a few minutes, a reply came in. "He'll meet us there. Ellie will drive him."

"Good." The chief gave a nod. "I think Mr. Finch's skills might be useful."

When they arrived at the Solana house, Chief Martin parked in front and they all emerged to see three police cars, an ambulance, and Solana's Chief Peterson and five officers standing outside speaking intently with one another.

The home was a good-sized white Colonial with black shutters and an attached two-car garage set back from the road on a slight incline. The grass was neatly mown and colorful flowers had been planted in the beds on either side of the front door.

A group of neighbors and onlookers stood across the street watching the commotion.

Peterson lifted his hand in a quick wave when he saw Chief Martin coming up the driveway. He gave a nod to the sisters. His face was pale and pinched. "The piece of firewood was taken from the stack out back in the yard. The young woman put the logs into the fireplace and lit them. As soon as she went back to the sofa, it exploded. Someone hollowed out the darned log and slipped a bomb inside of it. This guy is a monster."

Ellie's van pulled up and Courtney hurried to help Mr. Finch step out.

"I'm not going to stay. You don't need me," Ellie said.

Courtney smiled kindly. "It's fine, sis. Go on home. Thanks for bringing Mr. Finch. He'll go home with us." She slipped her arm through Finch's and the two moved slowly up the driveway to join the others.

"Another terrible explosion," Finch said clutching his cane in one hand. "Did the victims survive?"

"Chief Martin said they were alive when the

police arrived," Courtney told him. "The mother and daughter have been rushed to the hospital. I don't know what injuries they sustained."

Chief Martin thanked Mr. Finch for arriving so quickly and then said, "Why don't we all head to the rear of the house and take a look at the wood pile. A bomb squad is coming down from Gloucester to inspect the other logs. We won't touch anything. We'll just have a look. When Chief Peterson gives us the all clear, we can go inside and look around in there. He'll speak with us as soon as he can."

The small group went around the left side of the house to the backyard. The grass was lush, flowers bloomed in beds and in containers. There was a plunge pool, a patio, and a deck off the house extending out from four sliding glass doors.

The wood pile was off to the side behind a shed and two officers stood nearby to keep anyone from getting too close.

"We need to keep a ten-foot perimeter, Chief Martin," one of the officers warned. "No one is allowed any closer than that."

"Thanks. We'll respect the distance. We're just getting a look around."

"Whoever left the bomb in the log mustn't have counted on someone in the house using the wood any time soon," Angie said as she walked from side to side. "It's been hot. Not many people would be using a fireplace in the heat. It's a little cooler today, but not cool enough for most people to start a fire."

"The guy must be patient," Courtney said. "He probably didn't care if the wood was used now or three months from now. The result would be the same."

Jenna turned to the chief. "Could the bomb be outside for weeks in the heat and the rain without degrading?"

"If it was tucked well into the log, I don't think it would degrade. This area of the yard must be shady most of the time." The chief looked from person to person never really knowing how best to phrase his question. "Would you like to have some quiet time so each of you can try to pick up on anything out here?"

"That would be helpful," Mr. Finch said. "I'd like to get closer to the wood pile, but I suppose I'd be shooed away."

"You would," Chief Martin told him. "No one wants any more bombs going off. Keep a safe distance."

Finch moved to the patio and took a seat, closing

his eyes and opening his mind to anything that floated on the air.

Angie leaned closer to her sisters. "The guy could have planted this bomb weeks ago. It might have been the first one he left at a home. He's probably been waiting for a while for this one to go off. I doubt we'll sense anything from when he was back here."

Courtney said, "It's pretty bold to come into someone's backyard to hide a bomb. He must have done it at night when everyone was asleep. That would be the safest way."

"I wonder if there was only one bomb in that pile." Jenna took an involuntary step back.

"Let's hope so." Angie didn't intend to get any closer. "Shall we go off in separate directions to see if we sense anything?"

Jenna and Courtney nodded and moved off across the yard.

Angie stayed where she was, but turned in a small circle to get a feel for the place.

After ten minutes passed, Finch pushed himself out of the chair and went to speak with Angie.

"I don't feel anything. I wish I could put my hand on some of the logs in the pile. Maybe then I'd pick up something the bomber left behind."

"Maybe we can come back after the bomb squad inspects the wood," Angie said hopefully.

Finch frowned. "Unfortunately, the inspectors will handle all of the wood. They'll leave behind their own thoughts and intentions. That will contaminate the logs and will erase or disguise whatever the bomber left behind."

"When we go inside, maybe we'll be able to pick up on something," Angie said.

Jenna and Courtney came over to Finch and Angie.

"We didn't feel anything," Jenna informed the other two people.

Courtney narrowed her eyes. "This bomber must not be out to get anyone in particular. He must just be getting his kicks from random placements. Wherever it seems quiet with no peering eyes to see him as he goes about his wicked deeds is where he'll leave a bomb."

"The more bombs he delivers, the more unlikely it is that he's targeting certain people." Jenna let her eyes wander over the back of the house. "He can't have that many enemies."

Finch leaned on his cane. "The bomber must be obsessed with the adrenaline rush he gets from placing the bombs, and then he experiences another jolt of excitement when he hears one of his creations has gone off."

"Is he out to kill?" Courtney pondered. "Or is injury enough for him?"

"My guess is he would prefer a fatality," Finch surmised.

"I hope he doesn't keep trying for a death," Jenna said.

The chief came out from the sliding glass doors and waved his friends over. "We can all go in now. Please don't touch anything. The family room is covered in debris. Some of the ceiling came down, some furniture was destroyed, a window partially blew out. There's some blood here and there."

Jenna gripped Angie's arm.

"If you can't or don't want to go into the family room, do not feel forced to do so. Stay out in the hall or go into a different room," the chief told them. "Ready?"

The foursome followed the chief in a single file through the kitchen with its expensive cabinetry, countertops covered in granite, and polished, gleaming hardwood flooring. They moved past a huge living room, down a hallway into the expansive cathedral ceilinged family room. A large stone fireplace stood on one wall, and some of the stones had ripped out and fallen to the floor from the bomb. One window's glass hung from its casing. Shards of the glass sparkled on the floor in the afternoon sunlight.

Blood stains could be seen on the rug where one of the women must have fallen. The bright red blood on the white sofa stood out like a warning sign and the sight of it made Angie's stomach clench.

Jenna had to excuse herself to leave the house for some fresh air. The destruction was too much for her to bear.

Courtney whispered to Angie and Finch. "Someone sits in their basement building things that can cause damage and death? This is what's on the sick person's mind? To kill or maim or ruin?"

"Destroying things must be the man's obsession," Finch observed.

Courtney sucked in a long breath trying to calm her anger. "And now *my* obsession is finding this monster."

10

Angie stood at the kitchen counter mixing ingredients by hand in a big bowl, Mr. Finch sat at the island drawing in a sketchbook, Jenna was working on some jewelry designs in her notebook, and Ellie was reading at the kitchen table.

The cats sat on top of the refrigerator watching everyone and occasionally dozing.

When Courtney came in from the hall, she went to see what Angie was making. "What's cookin,' sis?"

Without looking up, Angie replied, "It's a Black Forest cake."

"Oh, yum." Courtney took a seat at the kitchen island to watch her sister. "I'm glad baking is a stress-reliever for you. It's win-win for all of us."

"The water in the tea kettle is still hot, Miss Courtney," Finch told the young woman as he lifted his cup to his lips.

Courtney made herself a cup of tea and returned to her seat. "That visit to bomb house number three was really disturbing. I can't stop thinking about it. That living room was a disaster. I keep picturing it in my mind."

"That's why Angie is making the cake," Jenna said. "We were all stunned by what we saw."

"I'm glad I didn't go. I don't have the stomach for it. I can't fathom cruelty." Ellie put her book down and went to get the platter of sliced apple cake which she carried to the island. She placed the slices on small white plates and served the family members who wanted some. "That's a beautiful picture," she told Finch.

Finch had sketched a few scenes of families outside their homes working or playing in the yards. Vivid colors were used to depict idyllic portraits of summer life in a small town with children playing, fathers mowing the lawn or performing other outside chores, mothers planting or tending flowers and vegetables, families eating lunch at picnic tables or playing games together on the lawns.

"The scenes are so pretty." Courtney leaned over to have a look. "I'd like to live in one of them."

Angie wiped her hands on her apron and came over to see the pictures as Finch turned the pages in his sketchbook. The third picture she looked at caused a cold chill to run over her skin and when she inspected it more closely, she was unable to find the cause of her odd feeling. Scrutinizing the drawing, she couldn't say why it bothered her, so she decided to keep her thoughts about it to herself.

"You're a very talented artist," Jenna told the older man. Finch had recently been invited by an art gallery in town to display some of his artwork, and he'd already sold two of his paintings.

"I love getting lost in a creation." Finch put down his drawings in order to eat his slice of apple cake. "It rests my mind and I'm able to make the world as I'd like it to be."

Angie smiled. "Baking does the same for me and I love making tasty things for people to enjoy. It makes me feel content and happy."

"It's a good thing we all have things we like to do so it takes our minds off of crimes," Courtney said. "I like watching the crime shows to try to solve the puzzles, but it's not the same as seeing the awful things people do to each other in real life. I got angry when we were at the bomb house ... it's all so stupid and senseless. Rufus and I are going for a long bike ride in the morning so it can help me clear my head. We need to buckle down and put our thinking caps on. We have to figure out who is making and placing these bombs."

"We will." Mr. Finch gave a nod. "The perp doesn't stand a chance with the Roseland and Finch gang on the case."

"I hope that's right," Jenna sighed.

"We haven't had a case beat us yet," Finch told them.

"And this one won't either." Courtney high-fived the man just as Tom came into the kitchen from the back door.

"Hello, all." Tom made a beeline for Jenna and wrapped her in a hug. "How's my wonderful wife?" He gently placed a hand on her stomach. "And how's our little baby doing?"

Jenna beamed at Tom. "We're both doing just fine."

"Sure smells good in here." Tom sniffed the air.

"Angie's making a Black Forest cake and we're eating an apple cake she made a little while ago." Courtney put a slice on a plate for him.

Tom made a cup of coffee and sat at the island

next to Jenna to eat his cake. "It was a long day. There's a new problem almost every day with that antique house we're renovating." Tom owned and ran a construction and renovation business. "Costs are adding up to more than what the owners hoped, but it can't be avoided." He went on to explain some of the issues and the plans to fix them.

"They're lucky they hired such a knowledgeable and experienced person." Jenna squeezed Tom's arm.

"A guy on my crew knows one of the bomb victims," he said. "Dennis Leeds."

"Really? What did he say?" Jenna asked.

"He told me Dennis is grateful he and his wife weren't hurt, but he's having trouble sleeping, his appetite is off, he isn't able to concentrate like he could before. He has nightmares about bombs and holding one as it explodes."

"Is he going to counseling?" Courtney asked.

"He hasn't yet. He will though." Tom took a swallow of his coffee. "Just the act of being targeted by the bomber is enough to throw people into a dark pit of anxiety. Leeds was lucky he didn't pick up that package, but I can see how the incident would terrorize you even if you weren't hurt."

Euclid and Circe stood up and hissed.

"Did Leeds share any ideas about who might have done it?" Jenna asked.

"He's suspicious of the guy who lives across the street."

"We heard about him," Angie said. "His name is Dave Hanes. He's unfriendly and gruff, doesn't interact with the neighbors and goes inside if anyone speaks to him or approaches him."

Finch spoke up. "Mr. Hanes might have social anxiety or some other reason he wants to be alone. I realize the behavior makes Mr. Leeds uncomfortable, but it isn't a reason to point a finger at the man without cause."

"That's very true," Tom agreed. "Chief Martin and his officers must be looking into any potential suspects in order to eliminate the ones who have alibis."

Ellie refreshed Tom's coffee. "I bet the chief will ask some of you to speak with Dave Hanes. The man might open up to people who aren't members of law enforcement. He might also feel more comfortable talking to people who don't live in the neighborhood."

"That's good thinking," Courtney praised her sister. "If the chief doesn't ask us to talk to Dave Hanes, maybe we should bring it up with him."

As Angie was removing the cake from the oven, her phone dinged with a text message and she asked Jenna to see who it was.

Jenna read the message and then slowly looked over at Ellie. "You did it again."

Ellie gave her sister a questioning look. "Did what?"

Putting a hand on her hip, Jenna explained. "The text is from Chief Martin. He wants two or three of us to meet with Dave Hanes. You knew he was going to ask us."

"I did not," Ellie protested. "I only thought it was a logical idea."

Courtney rolled her eyes. "Think what you want. You have this other skill whether you like it or not. Telekinesis *and* seeing the future. How come you get all the cool skills?"

Ellie's cheeks turned pink. "I cannot see the future."

"Maybe you can't *see* it," Courtney clarified with a smile, "but you sure *know* about it."

"It does happen fairly often, Miss Ellie," Finch said with a gentle tone. "I think it may be more than just logical thinking. You sometimes know when Chief Martin is coming here to the house."

Ellie became flustered. "You're all making more of this than it is. I *don't* know the future."

Courtney patted her sister's shoulder and kidded. "Maybe you don't know the future, but the future seems to know you."

"I'm going upstairs to take a shower." Ellie left the room in a hurry.

"Why can't I have her skills?" Courtney groaned. "I'd take them in a minute. They're just wasted on Ellie."

"When does the chief want us to talk to Mr. Hanes?" Angie asked.

Jenna reported the date and time.

"Can you come, Mr. Finch?" Angie asked. "I think your kind and easy-going manner might help to put the man at ease."

"I'd be happy to accompany you if Miss Courtney will handle the candy store."

"I'll handle the store. I think Angie's idea that you go to the interview is a good one."

Jenna offered to go as well. "Shall I reply to the chief?"

"Yes, please. Tell him my hands are a mess from baking and we'll meet him at Mr. Hanes's house tomorrow."

"Anyone want to watch a movie?" Courtney

poured some tortilla chips into a bowl and reached for the salsa.

Jenna, Tom, and Finch headed to the family room at the back of the house to relax on the sofas. The cats jumped down from the fridge and ran ahead of them.

"Let's choose a comedy," Jenna said. "I've had enough of crime for the evening."

Courtney carried the snacks on a tray. "You coming, Angie?"

"I'll be right there."

When everyone had left the kitchen, Angie took a seat at the island and gingerly reached for Mr. Finch's sketchbook. Opening it to the drawing he'd made that she'd looked at earlier, she peered at the picture trying to understand what there was about it that made her feel so uneasy.

A cold hard pit formed in Angie's stomach, her heart began to race, and a few drops of sweat trickled down her back as she slammed the sketchbook closed and hurried from the kitchen to join the others.

11

_____

When Dave Hanes opened the door, his expression was one of surprise even though he was well aware that Chief Martin and three consultants were coming to see him.

The man was in his mid to late thirties, had sandy blond hair that could use a cut, was around five feet ten inches tall, and had a medium build. He awkwardly led the way to the living room without introducing himself and moved away from the front door so quickly, no one had a chance to shake his hand or tell him their names.

Dave sat down first. He was wearing old, worn jeans and a short sleeved t-shirt. His fingernails looked dirty from oil or grease and Angie thought he might have been working on a car.

The guests took seats and the chief spoke.

"Thanks for talking with us." When he introduced Jenna, Angie, and Finch, Dave didn't seem to care what their credentials were or why they were sitting in on the discussion.

Dave looked expectantly from one to other, shifting a little in his seat so that he leaned forward with his hands folded between his legs.

"You were at home on the day your neighbor received a package bomb in his mailbox?" Chief Martin asked.

Dave nodded.

"Were you home all day?"

Dave nodded again.

"Were you outside when Dennis went to his mailbox?"

"I don't think so."

The chief tried to jog his memory. "Dennis Leeds thought he saw you in your driveway."

"He did? Maybe I was outside."

"Can you tell us what you were doing?" Chief Martin questioned.

"I don't remember. I don't remember seeing the neighbor." Dave's bottom lip twitched a little.

"Do you work, Mr. Hanes?" Finch's voice was light and easy.

"I'm starting back to work in a couple of days."

"What kind of work do you do?" Finch looked kindly at the man.

"I paint, I do some landscaping, some handyman kinds of things." Dave ran a hand over the top of his head.

"Do you work for yourself?"

"Sometimes, I do. I'm going back to work for a guy who owns a painting business."

"Have you worked for him before?"

Dave nodded.

"Were you unable to work for a while? Do you have an injury?"

"I was taking a break."

Finch nodded as if he understood perfectly.

Something about the man's answer picked at Angie. "How do you spend your day when you're not working?"

Dave straightened up. "I get up around 6am and eat breakfast. I watch the morning news. I clean the house or do some work in the yard. I've been working on my car. Then I eat lunch and watch the news. I exercise in the basement. I have some weights and a treadmill down there. Sometimes I take a nap in the afternoon. I like to read so I usually read some in the afternoon. In the summer, I work in the garden, then I make dinner and watch television."

"What kinds of books do you like to read?" Jenna asked.

"Murder mysteries and thrillers."

Jenna's breath caught in her throat.

"Do you have a favorite author?" Finch asked.

Dave listed a few popular writers.

Finch asked the man if he'd read a particular author hoping to chat a little about that writer in order to put Dave at ease, but he wasn't familiar with the name.

"Maybe I'll try one of his books sometime."

"Do you know the other people who live on this street?" Chief Martin asked.

"Not many. I know Dave Leeds because he was on the news about the bomb in his mailbox. I know some people from seeing them around."

"Do you talk with your neighbors when you run into them." Chief Martin held his stubby little pencil over his notebook.

Dave shook his head. "I don't like to talk to people I don't know."

Angie asked, "Do you have family in the area?"

"This was my parent's house. They're dead now. I inherited the house," Dave said. "I don't have anyone else."

Angie was beginning to feel sorry for Dave for his seemingly solitary existence when a white cat came into the room and jumped onto the man's lap. "What's your cat's name?"

"Snowball." Dave ran his hand over the cat's smooth fur.

"We have cats." With a smile, Angie told Dave about the family's two cats and he listened intently.

"Cats have strong personalities," the man said. "They're very smart."

Chief Martin guided the conversation back to the topic of the bombs. "Did you see anyone different on the street the day Mr. Leeds received the package?"

Dave blinked a few times considering the question. "You mean someone who doesn't live on the street?"

"That's right," the chief said. "Did you see anyone walking by that you didn't recognize? Did you notice a delivery person you've never seen before? Did someone drive around looking at the neighborhood?"

"I don't really remember the day. I'm not sure if I noticed anyone new." Snowball had his eyes closed and was purring loudly, and Dave gave the cat a sweet look. "What a minute. Maybe I did see someone that day."

Chief Martin, Angie, Jenna, and Finch held their breaths for a moment.

"Did you?" the chief tried to encourage Dave.

"I was outside in the backyard with Snowball. I take him out in the garden. He stays in the yard. I was weeding the garden and I noticed Snowball wasn't in back with me. I don't like him to be out of my sight in case a dog comes by." Dave rubbed at his forehead. "I went around to the front and Snowball was sitting in the driveway looking across the street. A car was parked in front of Dennis Leeds's house and a man got out. I scooped up the cat and we went back to the gardens."

"What did the man look like?" Mr. Finch asked.

"He had on a hat and sunglasses. He was wearing dark pants. They could have been dark jeans. He was wearing a white shirt ... a golf kind of shirt. He wasn't tall, he was like regular height. Not fat."

"How old was he?" Jenna questioned.

"My age, maybe? Thirties? I'm not sure. I only saw him for a few seconds."

"What did he do when he got out of the car?" the chief asked.

"I don't know. I went to the backyard." Dave gave a shrug.

"Was he carrying anything?"

"I didn't see. I didn't pay attention. He got out of the car as I was turning away from him."

"Okay. This is good information," Chief Martin praised the man. "Can you recall the time? What time was it when you saw him?"

"I work in the garden after lunch, but it's been hot out lately so I've been reading after I eat. So I guess it might have been around 2pm or so?"

"What kind of a car was it?" Angie leaned forward.

When Dave told them the color, make, and model, Angie's heart skipped a beat. "I don't know the year. It was maybe two or three years old."

"How do you know what kind of a car it was?" Jenna asked.

"I like cars."

"Did you notice any of the license plate numbers?"

Dave shook his head. "I notice cars, not license plates."

"Do you think the man in the car was a delivery person?" Chief Martin asked.

"Who knows?"

"A couple of officers have been here to talk to you," the chief pointed out. "You didn't mention the man or the car when they were here."

Dave narrowed his eyes and looked down at Snowball. "I didn't remember this when they were here."

"You just remembered today?" Angie leaned her head to the side.

Dave looked up. "The officers were rude."

"Were they?" Chief Martin's eyes hardened.

"They acted like I was dumb." Dave bit his lower lip.

"I'm sorry about that. I'll speak to them."

Angie brought up something they'd asked earlier in the interview. "Did you say you've been injured? Is that why you haven't been working?"

Dave looked her right in the eye. "I wasn't injured. The boss told me I had to take a few weeks off."

"Not enough work?" she asked.

Dave turned his head and looked out the window. "Me and another guy got into an argument."

"Did the other guy have to take time off, too?"

"No. He said it was my fault." Dave's jaw muscles tightened.

"Did you get into a physical fight?" Angie asked.

Dave moved around in his seat. "A little."

"What was the fight about?"

"I don't remember."

What's the name of the painting company you're going back to work for?" Angie asked.

"Blue Sky Painting." Dave looked up. "Do you want to see the gardens?"

Mr. Finch was the one who replied with a kind smile, understanding that Dave probably didn't have anyone to show his work to. "We'd love to."

With Snowball next to him, Dave led the small group down the hall and into the kitchen to the back door and into the yard.

The four people stepped outside and stood still, amazed at what they saw. Raised bed gardens full of vegetables and flowers covered the yard making it look like a garden store or a professionally-tended landscape. Tomatoes, peppers, carrots, lettuce, beans, and pumpkins grew in some of the beds and dahlias, impatiens, gladiolus, allium, asters, bee balm, black-eyed Susans, and tall sunflowers filled the other beds and some clay pots.

"You sure have a green thumb," Jenna gushed.

"It's remarkable," Mr. Finch told the man. "Amazing."

"You're a very talented gardener," Angie said.

Looking as proud as he could be, Dave walked them around the yard telling all about the plants and how he'd started most of them from seeds.

As she strolled around the paths, Angie thought back to the conversation they'd had inside the house, and a niggling feeling kept picking at her.

Was Dave telling the truth about the man and the car parked in front of Dennis Leeds's house?

12

"This is the room we want to use as the nursery." Jenna showed the room to Angie. It was next to her and Tom's master suite, had three big windows to let in lots of light, and was one of the smaller second floor rooms which made it seem cozy and perfect for a new baby.

"I think it's great. I've always liked this room." Angie stood by the windows and looked out to the street.

"I think we'll paint it a soft shade of cream and then add pops of color with accents like a rug, curtains, pictures on the walls, and bedding."

"Will the accent colors be pink or blue?" Angie tried to trick her sister into telling her if she was having a boy or a girl.

Jenna gave Angie a smile. "Nice try, but if I knew what we were having, I'd tell you. I don't want to know. We want it to be a surprise."

"Really? Then why do I have a feeling you know?"

"It's your imagination. I really don't know."

"Okay," Angie said. "If you *did* know and didn't tell me, it wouldn't seem fair since you know we're having a girl."

Jenna gave her sister a squeeze on the arm. "I swear I'd tell you if I knew."

Angie didn't give up. "Do you have a feeling one way or the other?"

With a laugh, Jenna shook her head. "Do *you* have a feeling about my baby?"

"Maybe. You tell me what you think first."

"No. It's another trick." Jenna led the way downstairs. She and Tom and sometimes, a hired worker had been working on restoring the old house for what seemed like ages. The living room, dining room, kitchen, and master bedroom were finished and beautifully done with shining hardwood floors, softly painted walls, high ceilings, and gorgeous cabinetry and granite countertops in the kitchen.

Jenna and Tom always said the house was going to bankrupt them before they ever finished it, and now with the baby coming, the renovation would slow to a crawl. Jenna had told Angie one day, "Maybe the house will be finished in time for the baby's graduation from high school ... or college."

While making tea in the kitchen, Angie asked, "Has Katrina been around lately?"

Jenna put some homemade brownies and some sweet and salty cookies on a plate. "She's around. Sometimes she's quieter than usual, but whenever I'm in the room the baby will have, I can sense her."

"Is she okay with the new addition?"

"She actually seems happy about it." Jenna took honey from one of the cabinets and sliced a lemon for the tea.

A ghost named Katrina Stenmark lived in Jenna and Tom's house, and there were times when she could be feisty or in a bad mood. One of Jenna's skills was the ability to see ghosts, but this particular spirit would not show herself. Despite never having observed Katrina, Jenna could feel her presence in the house and knew when the woman was in the same room with her. It took the young couple some time to adjust to having a third person living with them, but now it was second-nature and they would both miss the ghost if she ever decided to move on.

"I can feel Katrina's joy whenever I'm in the baby's room."

"I wonder if the baby will be able to see ghosts like you do." Angie bit into a cookie.

One of Jenna's eyebrows went up. "This is going to be interesting, isn't it? We'll have to watch these two little ones very carefully for any *special* abilities."

"Why didn't our skills show up until we all moved here to Sweet Cove? Is there something about the town that draws out a person's skills?"

"Or is it because Nana and some of our ancestors lived here? Is there some power around here that we tap into?" Jenna asked.

"Maybe it was because we were ready to accept our skills?"

"Hmm," Jenna said. "Ellie isn't ready to accept her skills, but the abilities still showed up in her when we moved here from Boston."

"Oh, right." Angie gave a chuckle. "I guess my idea that skills show up when you're ready for them is completely wrong." After taking a sip of her tea, she asked, "Do you think about Mom?"

Jenna sighed. "A lot. Especially when we got married and now that we're both expecting babies. I wish I could talk to her and ask her questions."

"Me, too."

"Do you ever wonder about how she died?" Jenna's tone was soft and quiet as if she was uncomfortable about bringing up the subject.

"I do wonder." Angie looked closely at her sister. "She died crossing a street in Boston on a sunny day ... a street that wasn't that busy. A hit and run. Knowing what we know now about our family and paranormal skills, do you think how she died is suspicious?"

Jenna answered with one word. "Yes."

"Maybe we need to look into this," Angie suggested. "We could talk to Orla about it. She might know something."

"If she knew something, why wouldn't she tell us?"

Angie cocked her head to the side. "Maybe we have to be ready to hear it."

"Let's talk to Courtney and Ellie and see what they think," Jenna said.

Angie finished the tea in her cup. "You know, something's been bothering me about our visit to Dave Hanes."

"What is it?"

"Could Dave have made up that he saw a man near Dennis Leeds's mailbox?"

"Why would he do that?"

"He might have decided he likes the attention he's getting and a lot of what he told us was mentioned in the news after Agnes Shield's neighbor gave the police the description of the man she saw leaving Agnes's porch. Dave might be mimicking that information. The whole thing might be making Dave feel important."

"He did mention seeing a car though," Jenna pointed out. "And was very specific about what kind of a car it was."

"Dave could be making that up." Angie shook her head slowly. "I don't like to be so suspicious, but when we're working these cases, I feel like we need to have reservations about what people are telling us. Initially, anyway."

Jenna blinked. "I believed him. Am I being naïve?"

"Probably not." Angie rinsed her cup in the sink and put it in the dish washer. "What did you think about him telling us he had to take time off from his painting job? He got into a fight with another worker? The boss made him take time away? Why didn't he just fire Dave?"

"That's a good question," Jenna agreed. "Why keep a troublemaker on the payroll?"

"Something keeps nagging at me about what

Dave told us. I don't know exactly what it is that's making me uneasy, but it's definitely picking at me. I think we should pay a visit to Dave's boss. Let's bring it up with Chief Martin. Maybe someone has already talked to the man."

Jenna ran her hand though her long brown hair. "There's quite a bit to sort through. I wish I could wave a magic wand and make everything right."

"Unfortunately," Angie kidded, "we can't locate our magic wands." A couple of seconds later, the grin dropped from her face. "When I was looking at the drawings Mr. Finch made the other evening, one of them made me feel nervous. Really nervous."

Jenna's face took on a serious expression. "Which drawing was it?"

"The third one in the sketchbook. There's a pretty house and some kids playing a game in the yard with their mom and dad. There's a small brown dog in it, too. Mature trees ring the sides of the property. A man is mowing the grass in the side yard and another man is on a ladder painting the house. Everyone is happy. Everyone seems to be enjoying themselves."

"Then what's the problem?" Jenna asked.

"All I know is every time I look at that picture, I feel anxious and afraid and I feel like I have to run away from it." Angie's heart had begun to race just thinking about the drawing.

"Did you tell Mr. Finch what effect the picture has on you?"

Angie shook her head. "I didn't. I don't know why I didn't."

"Talk to him about it. He might have some feelings about the drawing that match yours. Both of you can search for clues as to why you feel so uneasy when you look at it."

"I will. I'll tell him how I feel." Angie looked at her sister with worry. "Will our feelings of anxiety and fear and revulsion over the criminal acts we encounter hurt our babies?"

"Nah. These two kids are resilient." Jenna winked. "They have to be in order to be part of this family. We run into a lot of weird stuff."

Angie smiled. "I'm really glad we're going through these pregnancies together, especially since we don't have Mom around."

Jenna glanced up at the antique clock above the sink. "We'd better get ready to go. We don't want to be late."

"Let's hope Agnes Shield's husband has some insight into why their house was targeted," Angie said.

"And let's hope he didn't have anything to do with it." Jenna picked up the keys to the car and started for the door.

"Gosh." Angie's eyes widened. "I sure hope not."

"Like you said earlier, we shouldn't trust anyone."

13

Jenna pulled the car to the side of the road across from the Shield's home and before they could get out, a man in his thirties thumped on the passenger side window causing Angie to jump.

After Jenna put the window down, the man peered into the car. "Come on, lady. Don't park here." Looking to be just under six feet tall, the man was tanned, with dark blond hair, and was missing one of his teeth. His face was angry. "Can't you see we're painting here? Another truck is going to show up soon. We need to be able to move equipment into it."

Jenna felt annoyed by the man's rude behavior. "How did I know? You could ask nicer, you know."

She hit the button to make the window raise and pushed the ignition to bring the engine to life. After doing a three-point turn, she brought the car to a stop in front of the Shields' house.

As the sisters walked towards the driveway, Jenna grumped. "Why do people have to be so mean? Am I a mind reader? How was I supposed to know an equipment truck needed to park there?"

Angie glanced across the street at the painters working on the house. "Look. It's Blue Sky Painters. That's the company Dave Hanes works for. I don't see him."

"Maybe they have different teams working at different places." There was still an angry edge to Jenna's voice in reaction to being yelled at when she parked.

Everett Shield opened the door to the young women as soon as they stepped up onto the porch. "Hello," he greeted them warmly and introduced himself. "The living room is probably more comfortable. It's pretty humid out here."

The sisters joined the man in a nicely decorated living room with a fireplace on one wall and big windows looking out to the green lawn.

In his late seventies, Everett, tall, slender, and

white-haired, offered drinks to his guests and Jenna and Angie accepted glasses of seltzer.

"How is Agnes doing?" Angie had been worrying about her for days.

"She's doing remarkably well. She's a strong, resilient woman, always has been. She's the type of person who looks beyond the negative things of life and tries to find a silver lining." Everett gave a nod and a smile. "I'm lucky I found her ... and that she agreed to marry me."

"It sounds like Agnes's mental state is good," Angie said.

"She has her down moments when her spirits drop, but she bounces back. She's determined to return to her activities. Agnes knows she'll have to compensate for the loss of her fingers and she'll have to be patient. She's a fighter. Nothing slows her down for long. When Agnes sets her mind to something, she does it," Everett said with pride. "She's a heck of a woman."

"Did you see her today?" Jenna asked.

"I see Agnes every day. I told her you were coming to see me this afternoon and she asked me to give both of you her regards. She's moving to the rehab facility tomorrow. Another step in the healing process."

"How are you doing with all of it?" Jenna asked kindly.

Everett's face softened. "It's been a difficult experience. I'm not as positive a person as Agnes is. I appreciate and admire that characteristic in her. She's good for me. Her enthusiasm for life and her upbeat attitude lifts me. I'm not morose by any means. I'm not a negative person. It's just uplifting to have Agnes around. I miss her not being at home with me." Everett took a long swallow from his coffee mug. "What happened to my wife has been very disturbing. It's a violation of our lives. Someone had the nerve to invade our space and harm Agnes. His intent must have been to kill someone. It's absolutely alarming and unsettling for this to have happened. We're people who take pride in helping others. We try to be good people. I've been having trouble sleeping at night. I worry irrationally about Agnes. Sometimes, I think I hear someone dropping a package on the porch. I have to keep telling myself that things are okay."

"Do you think it would be helpful to speak with a counselor?" Angie asked gently knowing that many people wouldn't take the question well.

"In fact," Everett said, "I've just started this week.

I'm hoping it will be useful. Anyway, enough about me. How can I help?"

"We were told you weren't home on the day of the incident," Angie told him.

"That's right. I was away for a couple of days camping with a friend. When I got the call, we raced back as fast as we could."

"Are you still working?"

"Oh, yes. I'm a research scientist at the university. I have a degree in neuroscience. I study learning disabilities. I'm like Agnes. We both enjoy our jobs."

"Your neighbor next door believes she saw a delivery person leaving your front porch shortly before Agnes came outside and found the package," Angie said. "Did you hear Mrs. Lancer's description of the man?"

"I did hear."

"Does the description sound like anyone you know?"

"It's a fairly generic description. There's not a lot to go on. No one came to mind when I heard about it."

"We asked Agnes if there was anything that happened recently that would lead to someone planting the package at your house and she couldn't think of anything," Angie explained. "Do you recall anything? An argument? A disagreement? Do you remember Agnes relaying anything about an incident?"

Everett's forehead creased as he thought it over. "I don't remember anything like that."

"How about with you?" Jenna questioned. "Have you had any run-ins with anyone?"

"Me? No, I haven't. Nothing I recall." Everett's face flushed. "Do you think the bomb was intended for me? Was I supposed to pick it up?" The man ran his hand over his face. "Is someone angry with me for something? Was this thing directed at me? I had the idea it must have been random."

Angie told the man, "The police aren't sure if the packages were randomly placed or if people were targeted. They're still working to make a determination."

"Do you know any of the other people who have been involved?" Jenna asked. "Dennis Leeds, or the mother and daughter, Roberta and Sally Reynolds?"

"I don't know them. I don't think I've ever met any of them."

"What about Dennis Leeds's wife, Carol?"

Everett shook his head. "The name isn't familiar."

"Lincoln Reynolds?"

"No. That name isn't familiar to me either." Everett looked very fatigued. "All of these people live in Solana, correct?"

"That's right," Jenna said.

Everett said, "It's not a large town, but I haven't met any of these people. At least, I don't recall meeting them. What is the tie that binds them all together? Is there one, or are the incidents only related because they have the same perpetrator?"

"The police are working to find the answer." Angie nodded in an encouraging way.

"For now," Jenna said, "we'll assist by doing interviews and research so the police will have all the necessary puzzle pieces."

"Do you go camping often?' Angie asked.

"I love camping, being outdoors, the fresh air, having a campfire, cooking on a little gas stove. Agnes is not a fan of such things so I go with a friend of mine, maybe three times a year."

"Do you enjoy hiking?"

"Oh, yes. We hike for miles every day. We take the kayaks and go out on the river or the lake. If the water isn't too chilly, we'll swim." Everett had a wide smile on his face. "I wish Agnes enjoyed it. I've been telling her for decades that she's really missing something." The man chuckled. "Agnes always says if she went camping she'd *really* be missing some-thing ... her comfortable bed."

"I'm inclined to agree with her," Jenna smiled.

"Was your most recent camping trip planned well in advance?" Angie asked.

"It's necessary to plan ahead in order to get reser-vations. The camping areas often fill up months in advance." Everett's face fell and he stiffened slightly. "You ask because you suspect me?"

"I ask because we're trying to find the person responsible for trying to kill people."

Everett sighed. "I understand. Every part of this episode is so far out of our realm that it can be very jolting."

"I'm sorry some of the questions can be difficult," Angie apologized. "But they have to be asked."

After a few more minutes of conversation, the sisters thanked Everett for his help and cooperation and rose to leave. The man walked them to the door and when he opened it, Jenna noticed the rude painter across the street walking towards his truck. When he spotted them standing on the Shields' porch, the man gave them a look of disgust and got into his vehicle.

Jenna felt a surge of anger bubbling up inside. She gestured across the street. "We parked in front of that house when we got here. That painter was so rude to us."

Everett nodded. "He was rude to Agnes, too. He yelled at her one day over something ridiculous. Agnes told him where to go. She isn't someone who takes anyone's guff."

Jenna was fuming, remembering the painter's rudeness. "*I* should take a lesson from Agnes and tell that guy where to go."

14

Lincoln Reynolds was forty-nine-years-old with the body shape of a marathon runner. With brown-eyes and light brown hair cut close to his head, he gave off a sense of intensity as if he was never quite able to relax. The shadow of beard stubble showed over his cheeks and chin. He had either started growing a beard or he hadn't bothered to shave for a few days.

The man's wife, Roberta, and his seventeen-year-old daughter, Sally, were the ones injured in the fireplace bomb several days ago.

Chief Martin, Angie, and Jenna sat in the sunroom off the kitchen. Lincoln avoided the family room where the bomb had gone off and was having it repaired and renovated.

"How are they doing?" Chief Martin asked the man about his family.

"They're getting better. My wife suffered a concussion, some deep cuts that required stitches, a couple of broken ribs, and damage to her ear drums. The doctors are hoping the hearing loss will reverse itself over time. Our daughter is also suffering from hearing loss, she had to have surgery to her left eye due to flying glass, and she broke her left arm and leg from being thrown across the room from the blast." Lincoln seemed to deflate while talking about the injuries. "Things can change in a second, can't they?"

The chief nodded empathetically. From his work in law enforcement, he'd seen plenty to back-up the man's comment about how things could change in seconds. Not long ago, Chief Martin almost lost his life from being attacked with a syringe full of an opioid.

"We're assisting the Solana Village Police Department in investigating the package bombs," the chief said, "along with other federal agencies. You'll most likely be contacted to speak with several officers and detectives from those departments, if you haven't already. I apologize in advance if our questions overlap. I hope you'll bear with us."

"That's fine. I want to do what I can to help." Lincoln's face was lined with worry and his eyes were bloodshot from sleepless nights since the accident.

"Can you tell us where you were when the accident happened?" The chief took out his notebook. No matter how many times he was teased by the Roselands, he rejected their suggestions to use a tablet or a laptop to write his notes preferring the small, paper notebook and pen. "It helps me remember things better if I write them out."

"I was at work. I'm a senior vice president of information tech. I'm with a large firm over in Peabody."

"What about Roberta? Does she work?" the chief inquired.

"She's an optometrist. She owns her own practice."

"Your daughter, Sally, was still on summer break from school?"

"Sally will be starting her senior year of high school next week." Lincoln's face dropped suddenly realizing Sally might need to postpone her return to school for a few weeks. "When she's able," he corrected himself.

"Did anything unusual happen prior to the incident?" Chief Martin had a kind expression on his face.

"Unusual?" Lincoln was confused.

"Maybe an argument with someone? Maybe your daughter had a fight with a friend or a boyfriend? Did your wife tell you about anything unpleasant that happened at work with a patient or a colleague?"

Lincoln rubbed at his face. "Nothing like that. Sally doesn't have a boyfriend. She's tight with her friends. Nothing upsetting was going on. Roberta gets along well with her staff and clients. She didn't tell us anything was wrong. Everything seemed normal."

"Did anyone in the family get into a fender bender recently?" Angie asked.

Lincoln shook his head. "Aren't these bombs being placed at random? I've read the news, and as yet, no links have been found between the victims. Is that right?"

"That's correct," Chief Martin told him. "But it doesn't mean that links don't exist. There may be connections that haven't been uncovered yet."

"The bomb was placed in a hollowed out log in your wood pile," Jenna pointed out. "Did you hire someone to cut and stack the firewood?"

"We ordered firewood for the upcoming fall season," Lincoln said. "We ordered from the same place we always do. They deliver and stack the wood. We've dealt with them for years."

Chief Martin asked for the name of the business. "Although it's the same business you've used for years, there may be new employees working for them."

"What about landscapers?" Angie brought up the question to find out who else had access to the woodpile. "Do you employ a lawn service to cut the grass?"

"Yes, and again, we've used them for years. They aren't new to us." Lincoln told the chief the name of the landscaping company.

"Does anyone else enter your yard for any reason?" Jenna questioned.

"The water guy comes to read the meter once in a while. The oil company comes when the oil for our burner is low. They only need to access the side yard for those things. No one needs to enter the backyard."

"Has anyone trespassed? Have you caught anyone lurking nearby? Does a car sometimes drive by with a driver who seems to look around?"

Lincoln looked baffled by the questions. "I'm at

work most of the time. After work, I go to the gym or go for a run. When I get home, I work a little more or we watch a movie after dinner. Sometimes we sit by the fire pit out back. I'm not peering out the windows watching for intruders. We're relaxing after a long day."

"Have your neighbors noticed anyone hanging around with no reason? Have any of the neighbors had a run-in with anyone recently?" Angie asked.

"I haven't heard of such things. We're all professionals, we're all busy. We have an online neighborhood communication system though. No one has reported anything. There's been nothing sent out to notify us of anything concerning."

"Who brought in the firewood that was in the family room?" Chief Martin asked.

"I think Sally went out and filled the bucket. It was a cooler day than it had been and she wanted a fire going while they watched a movie. My wife took the afternoon off that day to spend with our daughter. This summer has flown by. Sally was going back to school soon. They wanted to have the afternoon together." Lincoln sighed and looked out to the yard full of flowers and trees. "I should have stayed home that day." He whispered and brushed at his eyes.

"There wasn't anything you could have done,"

Chief Martin reassured the man. "You wouldn't have been able to prevent what happened."

Lincoln turned to the chief. "Thank you for your kind words. I appreciate it. But, really? The whole thing makes me feel helpless. There was no way I could protect my family from this. Isn't that awful? Are we all at the mercy of madmen?"

There was no answer to that so everyone sat in silence for a few moments until the chief spoke. "We take precautions to keep ourselves safe. We lock the doors. We don't walk alone at night or in deserted locations. We keep our phones handy. But yes, the hand of fate is fickle and can strike out when we least expect it. We can only do the best we can."

The words caused a cold shudder to run through Angie and she subconsciously put her hand over her abdomen to protect her unborn daughter.

"Are there any clues as to who is doing this?" Lincoln asked.

"The investigation is proceeding as expected. There are many people to talk with and many things to follow up on. We have an excellent team in place, but there are details we're not able to share with the public."

Lincoln nodded and then shared an observation. "When something like this happens, people can behave oddly. Some of our friends haven't called to ask about Roberta and Sally. Some people at work seem to be avoiding me. A few colleagues ask about my wife and daughter, but they're stiff and uncomfortable and always seem like they want to rush away. It's almost as though we're tainted now, like there's some primal instinct to keep away from someone who might pass their bad luck on to others."

"When tragedy strikes, some people don't know how to behave," Angie said knowing from the experience of her mother's sudden death how difficult it could be for some people to deal with tragic or sad events. "They don't know what to say, so they say nothing. They don't want you to feel badly so they say as little as possible and then change the subject. I don't think they're being uncaring, it's just that they don't know what to say or do so they avoid the whole thing."

"That's probably true," Lincoln said. "Some of our friends have been terrific, sending over meals, sending flowers to the hospital, visiting Roberta and Sally, calling me to talk. There are others that, well, I thought I could count on them, but I've learned otherwise."

"Focus on the ones who are supportive," Jenna

said with a nod. "It sounds like you have some very good people around you."

"You're right. I have too much hurt to deal with right now to allow any more hurt into my life." A few tears gathered at the corners of Lincoln's eyes, but he brushed them away and cleared his throat. "I'm grateful that my family survived and will be okay. Please find this person and lock him up. Then no one else will have to endure what my family and our little town is going through."

15

A clear blue sky stretched overhead as the Roseland sisters rode their boogie boards on the waves. Josh, Tom, Rufus, and Jack stood on paddleboards sliding over the ocean further out from shore.

Mr. Finch, wearing his Hawaiian print swim trunks and matching shirt, sat on a beach chair next to Betty. Circe rested on the man's lap and Euclid squished in next to Finch on the chair. Euclid and Circe didn't care to get their paws wet so they avoided the water unless they were aboard Josh's sailboat, but the two felines enjoyed digging in the sand and watching the family members and friends frolicking in the sea.

The sun was lower in the sky and soft violet and

pink colors painted streaks below the clouds. The family considered the late afternoon and early evening the best time of day to come down to the beach. The air was still warm and the crowds had thinned out as people headed back to their homes, hotel rooms, and rented houses to clean up and get ready for dinner.

Angie and Jenna emerged from the waves laughing.

"We got dunked," Jenna explained to Finch and Betty. "A wave flipped us off the boards."

Betty looked concerned. "Should you be riding the waves? Carrying the babies?"

Angie picked up her towel from the blanket spread over the sand. "Our doctors gave us the all clear. We're just at three months. Later on in the pregnancies, we'll need to stick with yoga and light jogging, but for now, we're allowed to do water sports."

"Later on in the pregnancies," Jenna noted, "it will be winter and we won't be swimming anyway."

Chief Martin's wife, Lucille, lay on a blanket warming herself in the sun. "When I had my kids, my doctor discouraged exercise. Now we know that isn't healthy or helpful to delivery. As long as the exercise isn't too strenuous or could risk a fall, then I say go at it. Your muscles and cardiovascular system will be in better shape."

"We're both very careful," Jenna said. "We wouldn't go in the ocean if the waves were big."

Chief Martin took a shovel they'd brought to the beach and started digging a hole for the logs. Their dinner of corn on the cob, burgers, and veggie burgers would be grilled on the beach and served with potato salad, green salad, and a bean salad from the cooler. Another cooler was full of drinks and there would be cut-up fruit, a variety of cookies, and marshmallows to toast for dessert.

Dripping wet, the men carried their boards out of the ocean and made their way up the sand to help the chief with the grilling and set-up. A collapsible table was stowed in Ellie's van and Tom went to get it so the food and drinks could be served from it.

"I won the paddleboard race." Rufus beamed with pride. "It's the first time I beat Josh."

"He let you win," Jack teased.

"No, he didn't." Rufus was indignant, but checked with Josh. "Did you?"

With a laugh, Josh shook his head. "I should say I let you win so everyone will think I'm still the champ of the races, but you beat me fair and square."

"There should be a prize," Rufus said.

Courtney and Ellie came racing out of the surf and when they reached the blankets, Courtney put her arms around Rufus and planted a kiss on his cheek.

"That's your real prize." Finch winked. "But you've also won the admiration of your peers and that is all the prize you need."

"Well said, Mr. Finch." Rufus opened the cooler and set drinks on the table Tom had just unfolded.

After Ellie and Courtney had dried off and slipped on long t-shirts, they set out plates and glasses along with salad dressings and napkins.

"I'm starving," Ellie announced. "That food sure smells good."

Euclid and Circe trilled with their little noses up in the air taking in the smell of the grilling meat and veggies.

"It will be ready in a few minutes," Tom alerted them.

Lucille, Betty, Jenna, and Angie removed the salads from the coolers, lit two jar candles, and poured drinks for everyone while five men stood around the grilling pit watching the food cook.

Lucille chuckled. "Funny how men huddle around an outside grill together like they're cavemen."

"Evolution takes time," Courtney smiled. "They're still subconsciously connected to their early ancestors' behaviors."

"It's fine with me," Ellie said, "this way I don't have to cook tonight."

Angie sat down next to Mr. Finch's chair. "Have you been drawing lately?"

Finch twirled his cane in the soft, white sand. "I have. It's a pleasant way to spend some time."

"When we were all in the kitchen the other evening and you showed us some of the sketches, one of them made me feel funny."

Finch pushed his eyeglasses up his nose and gave Angie a look. "Funny how, Miss Angie?"

"Something about it made me feel anxious, nervous, almost panicky."

"Which picture made you feel that way?"

Angie described it. "All the drawings have the same theme though and they all gave me an odd sensation."

Finch stroked his mustache. "I've been almost obsessed with creating those pictures of people outside in their yards enjoying themselves. They seem innocent initially, but there's something lurking underneath that causes me to feel unsettled."

Josh called out. "Dinner is served."

Finch leaned towards Angie and lowered his voice. "Shall we go through those drawings together some evening? Put our heads together and figure out why the pictures bother us?"

"I think that's a great idea." Angie stood and brushed the sand from her butt. "Do you think this has something to do with the bomb case we're working on?"

"I have a strong feeling it does, Miss Angie."

After the meal was eaten and dessert was served and the sun had disappeared over the horizon, the cats, Angie, Jenna, Courtney, Mr. Finch, and Chief Martin sat in the beach chairs in a little circle while the others made mixed drinks and stood with marshmallows on sticks held over the fire. Tom and Josh had set the tiki torches around the gathering spot and the warm, yellow glow lit up their little part of the beach.

"What did you think about the interview with Lincoln Reynolds?" the chief asked.

Angie said, "At first, I considered him a suspect, but after talking with him, I'm convinced he had nothing to do with it."

"I felt the same way," Jenna nodded and took a sip of from her glass of seltzer. "He seemed sincere in his feelings for his family and how the incident has upset him so much."

"I agree." Chief Martin bit into a cookie. "What about the painter, Dave Hanes, the man who lives across from Dennis Leeds, the man who spotted the bomb package in his mailbox? The guy is a loner, won't interact with the neighbors, was given a few weeks off from his job for fighting with a co-worker. I wonder if he bears some grudges and has allowed them to fester."

"The longer we talked to Dave, the more I liked the guy." Jenna zipped up her sweatshirt to ward off a chill. "But when we learned Dave had fought with someone at work, it worried me."

Angie said, "I had the idea Dave might be lying about seeing the delivery man and the car near Dennis Leeds's mailbox. Most of that information was in the news. He added the part about the car, but he could have made that up to seem important."

"The other thing I recall," the chief said, "was Dennis Leeds told us he saw Dave Hanes watching from his driveway when Dennis went to his mailbox, but Dave told us he wasn't outside at the time. One of them is mistaken."

"I forgot about that," Courtney told them. "What kind of detective consultant am I?"

"We all forget little details," Chief Martin said. "That's why I keep my notebook with me all the time. It helps to jog my memory."

Ellie came over to the group to give each of them a blanket and then she sat down with them. "How are things going with the case?"

They took turns giving her the updates.

"I can see how the bomber gets away with placing the bombs on Agnes Shield's porch and in Dennis Leeds's mailbox," Ellie said. "He dresses like a deliveryman and probably moves efficiently to make it seem like he needs to get his deliveries done in a timely manner, when in reality, he's moving fast to plant the bomb and get away. People see him and he doesn't make them suspicious. We all get deliveries now. It's a commonplace sight. But the bomber must have gone into the Reynolds's backyard at night. It wasn't a simple drop off of a package. He had to hollow out a log in order to place the bomb inside of it. That would take some time. Or did he find a log somewhere, prepare the bomb at his home, and then deliver it at night to the Reynolds?"

"I'd vote for prior preparation of the log," Angie said, and the cats trilled at her.

The others agreed.

"It would take too long to do the preparation on the premises," Finch said.

"So this log-bomb proves that the bomber knew the Reynolds had a wood pile in the yard," Ellie said. "He was familiar with what the logs looked like. He found one somewhere that wouldn't stand out from the others and he turned it into a bomb. My question is ... how did the bomber know about the wood pile? You can't see it from the street, right?"

"That's right," the chief said. "The wood is at the back of the yard. You can't see it when driving or walking by the house."

"That's my point," Ellie said. "The bomber had to know the wood pile was back there. He had to have been in or outside of that house to know the wood was there. He had to have seen it in daylight."

The others stared at her.

"The bomber isn't choosing his victims at random," Ellie pointed out. "He's choosing these particular victims for a reason."

16

Angie and Chief Martin walked into the small office of Blue Sky Painting to meet the owner, Bruce Brown. The man was in his late-forties, had tanned skin, blond hair, and blue eyes. He was wearing jeans and a blue Polo shirt with the name of his company embroidered over the pocket.

"Have a seat," Bruce told Angie and the chief. "How can I help you?"

The chief said, "From our phone discussion, you know we're assisting the Solana police with the package bomb investigation. We want to talk to you about one of your employees."

Bruce sat up straight, his eyes wide. "My employees? Is one of them involved in this mess?"

"We're not charging anyone and we aren't suggesting one of your employees is a suspect." Chief Martin made sure the man didn't think one of his workers was a bomber. "When we speak to or about someone, it might be because that individual can help us with the case. They may know something that seems trivial to them, but is actually an important clue to solving the case."

Bruce looked slightly relieved.

"One of your employees lives across the street from the second targeted individual. His name is Dave Hanes," the chief said.

One of Bruce's eyebrows went up. "Dave?"

"We spoke with Dave recently," Angie informed the business owner. "He was helpful."

"Can you tell us a little about Dave?" Chief Martin asked.

Bruce took in a deep breath. "Dave is a hard worker. He's a meticulous painter which comes in handy with trim work and detail work."

"How long has Dave worked for you?"

Bruce calculated in his head. "Three years? Off and on."

"Why off and on?" Angie asked. "Does he leave the job on occasion?"

Bruce looked uncomfortable. "Like I said, Dave's

a good worker. Sometimes, he can be hard to get along with. Sometimes, he irks the other workers. Some guys don't like Dave. I have to be careful who I pair him up with."

"What makes him hard to get along with?" Angie asked.

It took Bruce a few moments to answer. "Well, Dave is sort of a loner. That might not be the right description of him. He's better one on one. He seems to like to talk, but he doesn't like being in a group. Some of the guys can be crude. Dave doesn't like that and sometimes he speaks up about it which doesn't go over well with the others. It's hard to juggle the different personalities."

"Has there ever been trouble between Dave and some of the others?" Angie asked for clarification.

"Yeah." Bruce rubbed at his chin. "A guy who's worked for me for about five years can also be difficult. Joe Boles. He gets along great with the other guys, but he likes low, off-color humor so he gets the guys going with his talk. If Dave is around, he gets offended. One day, Dave raised his voice at Joe, called him some names. Joe has a temper, he can be a real grouch, moody. Joe pushed Dave, Dave pushed back. Some blows were landed. I didn't see it happen. Some of the other workers told me Dave threw the first punch. I made him take a few weeks off. I have to be sure to keep Dave and Joe off the same work team."

"Did Joe Boles work at a house across the street from the first bomb package victim? Her name is Agnes Shield."

Bruce looked surprised. "Yeah, we had a team there painting the interior and exterior."

"My sister and I parked in front of that house the other day," Angie told him. "A man was very rude to us. In so many words, he told us to get the car out of there. He implied we were stupid."

Bruce rolled his eyes and blew out a long breath. "I've talked to Joe a million times about not being rude to the neighbors. Unfortunately, he forgets what I've told him. I'll speak to him again about his behavior. I apologize. Please pass my apologies on to your sister." The business owner shook his head. "See what I have to deal with on a daily basis? If the guys aren't swearing at each other or throwing punches, they're talking rudely to the neighbors. It's a wonder any painting gets done at all."

Chief Martin said a few sympathetic words.

"Does Dave tell the truth?" Angie asked.

"The truth?" Bruce seemed confused. "I guess so. The conversation between the guys isn't anything high-level. The things I ask the guys don't lend themselves to lying. I'd be hard-pressed to know who tends to lie and who doesn't, so I can't help you there."

The chief asked, "Do you know if Dave has ever been involved in other episodes of physical fighting, either here or outside of work?"

"Not here, he hasn't. Just verbal arguments at times. I've never noticed him coming to work with a black eye or other injuries that would indicate he'd been in fights outside of work. Joe can push people's buttons. A sensitive guy like Dave can have trouble holding back when he's angry."

A chill ran over Angie's skin. *Trouble holding back when he's angry.* With a sinking heart, Angie wondered what else Dave could do if he was angry with someone.

~

ANGIE FELT fatigued and worn out when she got home after the interview and went straight up to her and Josh's apartment on the upper floor of the Victorian. Euclid and Circe greeted her at the front door and followed after the young woman when she climbed the stairs to her rooms.

"I'm tired," she told the cats. "I think I'll take a quick nap."

Angie changed clothes and crawled into her big, cozy bed with the two felines jumping up to join her. Euclid got comfortable at the foot of the bed and Circe used her front paws to knead at the blankets, purring loudly.

Angie smiled at the purring. "How can I sleep with all that racket?" she asked the black cat.

It turned out that Angie could sleep very well despite the noise of the purrs filling the air ... as soon as her head hit the pillow, she was deep in slumberland.

Josh had to be at work late that evening, but Jenna came looking for her sister.

Angie had left the door to the apartment open and Jenna entered with a knock. When Angie didn't answer, her twin went to see if she was having a nap.

Seeing Angie in bed with the two protective cats on either side, Jenna had to smile. Euclid lifted his head and seeing Jenna, he stood and stretched and jumped off the bed to greet her.

Petting the huge orange boy, Jenna whispered. "How long has sleepyhead been out?"

Angie shifted under the covers.

"Angie? You okay?" her sister asked.

Rubbing at her eyes, Angie yawned. "I'm fine, just exhausted. My body ran out of gas."

"It happens. Did you eat dinner?"

"As soon as I got home, I collapsed in here. I'm hungry now though." When she pushed herself up and got out of bed, Circe and Euclid led the way out of the room and down to the kitchen where Angie looked in the refrigerator for leftovers while Jenna made some tea.

She heated some spaghetti with vegetable sauce in the microwave, took a seat at the kitchen island to eat, and told Jenna about talking with the owner of Blue Sky Painting.

"That was nice of him to apologize for his employee's rude behavior towards us." Jenna sipped her hot tea. "The teams of guys sound like a bunch of kids from middle school, arguing, fighting, throwing punches. Why don't they just paint and keep their comments in check?"

"Good luck with that," Angie said. "I almost pitied the owner for having to deal with all their nonsense."

"Why didn't the owner make the bad-tempered guy take time off from work like he made Dave?" Jenna asked.

"The guy's name is Joe. The owner hinted that

Joe wouldn't have handled it well if he made him take a couple of weeks off, and anyway, Dave was the one who threw the first punch."

Mr. Finch came into the kitchen from the back door carrying a portfolio under his arm and he greeted the two young women.

"Is this a good time, Miss Angie?"

"Yes." Angie asked Finch to sit next to her.

"What are you two doing?" Jenna asked.

Angie reminded her sister how Mr. Finch's drawings had been causing feelings of unease and anxiety for both of them. Finch removed his sketchbook from the portfolio case and placed it on the island.

"Shall we just page through it?" Finch asked, and when Angie nodded, he opened the cover to the first picture.

The colorful drawings had the same themes, family and friends playing or working outside in the yard. The weather was perfect with blue skies and sunny days, and there were cheerful expression on the people's faces enjoying the weather and their companions.

"Why do these pictures bother you?" Jenna asked while peering closely at the scenes. "I like them. Everything looks perfect. Everything looks fun and happy."

"They look that way, but that's not what Mr. Finch and I feel from them." Angie could feel her heart beginning to race.

Finch kept turning the pages.

Angie's eyes widened. "You've done so many more of these."

"I pick up my colored pencils and pastels and the scenes pour out of my hand. I get lost in the drawing of them. It's almost like an obsession." Finch swallowed. It was clear he didn't like what was happening with the artwork. "Do you feel particularly influenced by one of the pictures?"

"Not really. My mind is confused." Some perspiration showed on Angie's forehead. "My thinking is so muddled. I feel like I want to get away."

Finch slammed the cover of the sketchbook. His breathing was coming fast and shallow. "Will you take the book away, Miss Jenna? Put it in the sunroom, please."

Jenna snatched it up. "Are you okay?" she asked her sister.

Angie nodded. "I'll be fine in a few minutes."

Jenna looked to Finch with worried eyes. "Mr.

Finch. Are you feeling okay? Do you need anything?"

"I'm fine. I think we'll feel better once we have a break from the sketchbook."

Jenna quickly carried the book out of the kitchen.

"Shall I destroy the pictures, Miss Angie?" Finch's voice was shaky.

Angie reached for the older man's hand. "Definitely not."

17

The waves crashed onto the sandy beach below the bluff at Robin's Point. A full moon lit up the area and made the night seem like day. A soft, warm breeze lifted the ends of Angie's hair for a moment before the strands fluttered back into place.

While Josh finished up in his office in the resort hotel, Angie took a walk over to the bluff to have a few minutes alone in the spot that meant so much to her family. As little kids, the Roseland sisters spent many happy summers at the Point with their nana in her cottage before the town took back the land and the small houses that had been built on it.

Josh owned the acreage on Robin's Point as part of the extensive resort grounds and he'd returned four parcels of that land to the Roselands. Angie and her sisters always felt close to their nana whenever they were on the Point, and on this evening, Angie needed to feel that sense of connection and closeness.

The package bomb case was taking a toll on her. The cruel intentions of the bomber seemed especially hard to handle even though every case they'd helped Chief Martin with had been difficult. Angie wondered if carrying a child made her more sensitive to acts of brutality or whether working on so many cases exposing the underbelly of humanity was wearing her down. She guessed it was both. Placing her hand on her abdomen, she closed her eyes and cleared her mind to ask her grandmother for the strength she needed to do what was necessary.

Angie listened as the delicate breeze moved through the leaves of the trees. She heard the power of the ocean as the waves hit the shore below, retreated, and crashed onto the beach, over and over again. Over time, the surging water could eventually erode cliffs and turn that mighty stone into pebbles. She had to remember that things took time, but that one day, strength and patience and determination would prevail.

Warmth ran through Angie's veins as she thought of Nana, and her mother, and her daughter and hope fluttered in her chest like the wings of a bird.

"Angie." Josh walked towards her over the grass and gently put his arm around her shoulders as he gazed at the silvery path the moon shined over the sea. "It's such a beautiful night."

Angie slipped her arm around her husband's waist and rested her head against his shoulder. "We're lucky, aren't we?"

Josh kissed the top of her head. "I know I am ... because I met you."

Hand-in-hand, they walked back through the beautifully landscaped resort grounds to the cottage they owned tucked away amidst the lush greenery. Because Josh worked such long hours and often needed to be on-hand at a moment's notice, the couple kept the cottage for convenience, but thought of their apartment in the Victorian as their real home.

After making tea, Angie and Josh sat together on the sofa and Josh handed her some brochures. "A sales consultant from a Boston-based children's furniture and accessories store was staying here for a few days. When she heard we were expecting a baby, she left these for us to look at."

Angie paged through the brochure. "This crib is really pretty."

Josh told her about the company's reputation for style and quality.

A second later, her eyes popped. "Did you see the prices?"

"Do you think it's too much?"

"It's outrageous. You could send a child to college for the cost of this crib."

Josh smiled at Angie's comment. "The price is for the entire room of furniture, not just for the crib."

"It's still too much. How long before Gigi outgrows this stuff and needs an actual bed and dresser?"

"I thought the things were nice. I want something nice for our daughter."

"They are nice, but we'd do our daughter a bigger favor by putting money away for her in a savings or investment account." Angie pointed out.

"We can do both ... buy the furniture and start an account for her."

"We're going to need to furnish a nursery here in the cottage and one in the Victorian. I think it's wasteful to spend so much," Angie told him. "I don't like to throw money away. No one knows what the future holds. How about we look for furniture that's pretty and doesn't carry the price tag of a small house?"

Josh chuckled.

"There's a new shop in town that carries beautiful things at a fraction of the cost," Angie said. "Let's look there."

"I'm going to want to spoil her, you know." Josh rested his hand over his wife's tummy.

"Spoil her with love and attention. Those are the things that matter and the things that she'll remember."

With a wide smile, Josh let out a sigh. "How is it that you're always right?"

~

ANGIE WAS asleep on the sofa and Josh was in the easy chair watching a movie when Angie's phone buzzed with an incoming text. Josh glanced at the phone on the side table and sat up fast. He stood and went to his wife, softly speaking her name.

Angie's eyes opened. "Is it time to get up?"

"It's only 9pm. You were napping." Josh ran his hand over her cheek. "Chief Martin just sent you a text. I think you need to look at it." He handed the phone to Angie.

Pushing herself up to sitting position, Angie rubbed at her eyes and took a look at the message on the phone. "Oh, no." Her fingers flew over the screen to send a reply.

"Will you come with me?" she asked Josh.

"Of course. I'll change out of my sweatpants." Josh hurried into the bedroom while Angie made a call to Jenna.

"Jenna will meet us. She's going to ask Mr. Finch and Courtney to come, too," she told her husband as she slipped on jeans and a sweater. "When is this going to end? When will someone figure it out?"

Josh wrapped her in his arms for a few moments, and then they left the cottage and went to the car to drive to the address in Solana Village.

"Did the text say anymore?" Josh asked as he turned the car south.

"Only that there'd been another bomb. He asked if we could come and he gave me the address." Angie hadn't had time to brush her hair so she pulled it up into a ponytail.

"Any word on the victim?"

"No, the chief must have been in a hurry." Angie looked out the window at the dark sidewalks punctuated with small, blotches of light from the street-lamps. As they drove, she told Josh more about the meeting with the owner of Blue Sky Painting. "Dave Hanes has trouble controlling his emotions."

"Maybe a pop in the face was just what the other guy needed."

"The other guy's name is Joe Boles. I think Dave hitting him only upped the bad feelings between them. Joe sounds like a troublemaker and seems to know how to push Dave's buttons. The two of them can't work on the same team anymore."

"Better to keep them apart," Josh agreed. "I'd probably let them go, but I don't have as much trouble hiring and retaining good workers for the resort. I had a friend who owned a roofing company. He was a nice guy, he treated his workers really well. He'd hire people and they'd collect one pay check and then they'd be gone, never to return. It happened all the time. He was constantly training people."

Angie reported how she and Finch experienced bad feelings when looking at the drawings the older man had done. "Mr. Finch said he has the urge to draw the same themed-pictures over and over. It had become concerning to him, but now we know it's some kind of clue. We'll go over the new ones again in a few days. There's a message in the pictures. We just have to figure out what it is."

Josh turned the car into a well-tended neighborhood of smaller Capes and ranches. Flashing lights could be seen up ahead and police cars were positioned to block off the road. An officer approached the car and Josh put down the window.

"You can't go any further," the officer said. "You'll have to turn back around."

Angie recognized the officer and leaned over the console. "It's me, Angie Roseland. Chief Martin of Sweet Cove asked me to come."

"Oh, Ms. Roseland. I didn't see it was you. If you pull to the curb and park, you can walk to the house where the chief is waiting."

Josh parked and they walked together towards the flashing lights. A sharp odor carried on the air and made Angie's nose sting.

"There's a fire up ahead," Josh said.

A ranch house was fully engulfed in flames. Angie and Josh crossed to the other side of the street and walked up the sidewalk to a group of neighbors watching the commotion.

A neighbor said, "The car is on fire. They won't let us get any closer in case it explodes. The firefighters have almost got it out. The house is another story."

One person said, "I was watching television. I heard an awful blast. When I looked out the window, I saw Jesse and Mary's car on fire. It spread to the house."

Angie's heart pounded. "Jesse and Mary are the owners? Did they get out of the house?"

"They're fine. They're with the police officers," someone else said.

"Shall we cross to the other side to find Chief Martin?" Josh asked.

Angie's eyes swept over the inferno in front of her. Angry orange flames shot into the sky and plumes of smoke created black clouds that drifted away from the scene.

Angie tugged the front of her sweatshirt up over her nose to keep from inhaling the smoke and she reached for Josh's hand. "I think I'd like to wait for my sisters and Mr. Finch."

18

"Ellie is sure the bomb victims are chosen deliberately, not at random," Angie said. "And I'm inclined to agree with her."

Jenna, Courtney, and Mr. Finch sat in the Solana Village Police Station conference room with Chief Martin. Josh went back to the cottage and Jenna would drive Angie home after they were finished with the meeting.

The young homeowners were in another room being interviewed by a detective and when they were done, Jesse and Mary Foley would speak with the sisters, Finch, and Chief Martin.

Angie explained the reasoning behind the thinking that the bombs were not being placed at random, and Chief Martin told the small group that he'd been leaning that way himself.

"Someone had to see the pile of firewood in the rear yard of the Reynolds's house," Jenna said. "We should drive on the road that loops around behind the Reynolds's property to see if the firewood is visible from the street."

"I did that the other day," the chief said. "I wasn't doing it to see the pile of wood, but I don't think you can see it from back there. I'll take another drive by tomorrow."

"So if the bomber is deliberately targeting certain people, what's the connection between them?" Courtney asked.

"The connection may not be obvious." Finch rested both hands on top of his cane. "The bomber may have strange reasons for picking these people out. Maybe one of them cut him off in traffic, maybe someone at work annoyed him. The reasons may not be based in reality."

"Those are good points." Jenna nodded. "We have to consider that the bomber could be choosing victims from all aspects of his life, from the cashier at the grocery store to someone he meets in passing. It's not going to be a simple task to link the victims to the bomber."

A knock came on the door and two people in their late-twenties entered the room. Mary Foley was slim and petite with shoulder-length auburn hair. Her eyes were red from crying. Jesse Foley was about five feet, ten inches tall with dark brown hair and brown eyes. They both had on jeans and t-shirts. Jesse was wearing sneakers and Mary had on a pair of flip flops.

Chief Martin said, "I know you've had to tell about the evening many times already, but I need to ask you to go through it once again as if you haven't told the story to anyone."

Jesse ran his hand over the top of his head. The couple showed signs of fatigue and shock, their faces drawn and serious, their eyes wide, shoulders slumped, both looking uncomfortable and nervous. An officer brought in cups of coffee and some cookies and put them on the table.

"I was working in the basement. I like to do woodworking. A huge blast shook the house. Mary called down the stairs to the cellar to me."

"I was in the kitchen. At first, I thought Jesse had done something downstairs to cause the explosion." Mary wrung her hand together. "Then I saw the fire outside the window. I screamed to Jesse and he came running upstairs."

"I worried something happened in the kitchen, maybe the stove exploded or something. When I saw the car, I couldn't believe it."

"We have a remote starter," Mary said. "I used it to start the car when I was in the kitchen. I'd been hot all day and I wanted the air conditioning to start up before I got in the car. I didn't connect the explosion to the car right away."

Jesse said, "We were both in shock. I called the fire department and when I finished the call, the neighbor from across the street was yelling and banging on our front door. He told us to get out of the house. He was afraid the car would blow up and he said the flames had already spread to the house. We grabbed our keys and wallets and ran."

"We waited in the neighbor's house. I started to cry. I told Jesse I caused the explosion by using the remote starter." Mary dabbed at her eyes.

Jesse took in a deep breath. "The remote starter didn't cause this fire. There was nothing wrong with the car. It was brand new. We bought it a few weeks ago. It was that bomber. He must have put a bomb somewhere near the engine. It must have been set to blow when the car started. If Mary didn't use the remote starter, well, she would have...." His voice trailed off.

"I'd be dead," Mary managed to squeeze the words from her throat.

Jesse took his wife's hand in his. "We're very lucky. Of course, not from the standpoint of losing our car and house and most of our things, but we have each other and we're alive. I'm very grateful." The man's eyes misted over.

Mary gently touched the man's cheek.

"It's not yet known if a bomb caused the explosion," Chief Martin explained. "It will take some time for that determination to be made."

Jesse nodded. "The other officers told us that. I know no one can jump to conclusions, but in my heart, I know it was a bomb."

Angie asked, "Is there a reason you feel you've been targeted? Did something happen recently that makes you suspect a bomb?"

"Only the other bombs that have been placed in town," Jesse said "and a car doesn't usually blow up on its own."

"Did either of you have trouble with someone over the past few weeks?" Jenna asked.

"No." Jesse looked at Mary. "We can't remember anything happening that would make someone so angry with us that they'd plant a bomb."

"What if you remove the idea that an incident

would have to be something big to cause this?" Finch asked the couple. "The bomber may perceive things in a distorted way. He may blow things out of proportion ... things that someone else would dismiss and forget."

Mary bit her lower lip thinking about what Finch had said.

"I can't think of any reason to target us." Jesse helplessly shrugged a shoulder.

"What do you do for work?" The chief asked.

"I'm a chef at a restaurant in Silver Cove. This was my first night off in weeks." Mary's expression was one of disbelief at what had occurred.

Jesse said, "I'm an accountant. I work in Salem."

"Have any of your customers or clients been upset or angry over anything in recent weeks?" Courtney asked the question.

Both Jesse and Mary shook their heads.

"Any complaints from someone? Any pushy or excessively demanding customers?" Courtney tried to prompt a memory.

"Nothing out of the ordinary," Mary said. "There are always demanding diners. There are always a few complaints. We make them right and the customer is satisfied."

Jesse reported no complaints from any clients at the accounting firm.

"Have either of you been involved in a traffic issue? An accident? A fender-bender?" Courtney tried to jog the young couple's thoughts.

Again, the answer was no.

"Any disagreements with colleagues?" Jenna asked.

"No. None."

"What about with a neighbor or with the oil company, the electric company, anything like that?" Angie questioned.

"We can't think of anything," Jesse told them.

"Do you have family in the area?" Mr. Finch asked.

"We're both from Virginia," Mary said. "We have some friends we can stay with."

Jenna had to clarify what she'd meant. "Do you have any family members with whom you don't get along?"

"Oh," Mary said. "I see what you mean. We get along with our families. There isn't a weird uncle or a strange brother or anything like that. No one from our families resents us or dislikes us."

"Have you noticed anyone suspicious in the neighborhood?" the chief asked.

Mary's hand went to her throat. "That scares me."

"I haven't noticed anyone around," Jesse said and then looked at the chief. "If it *was* a bomb, when could it have been planted? He'd have had to do it this evening, wouldn't he? If it was set to go off when the engine started? He must have been out there when I was in the basement. He must have been quick." The young man's face reddened with anger.

Chief Martin asked if the couple knew any of the other targeted individuals and listed off their names.

"I don't know them," Mary said.

"Neither do I." Jesse's disgust and anger seemed to be increasing the more he had to talk about the incident.

"You've both experienced an unexpected, tragic loss," Mr. Finch pointed out. "It is difficult to come to terms with such things. It might be helpful for you to talk out your emotions with a counselor or your doctor." Finch made eye contact with the young man and woman. "You've lost your car, your home is damaged, you came close to a calamity that might have taken your lives. This can lead to feelings of loss or a feeling of being unsafe. It is not a sign of weakness to see someone for assistance. An experienced professional can walk you through the grieving process and help you handle the situation emotionally. Please consider talking with someone about what has happened. It's important to take care of yourselves."

The couple nodded and Mary thanked Finch for his suggestion.

Feelings of unease had been pulsing through Angie's veins. She had the feeling the couple could help with a clue, but she didn't know what else to ask. Even though everything seemed to have been covered during the conversation, Angie didn't want them to leave. "If you remember anything that's happened over the past few weeks, would you call one of us? No matter how trivial it may seem. The smallest detail can end up being the answer we're all looking for."

The chief thanked the couple for their time and wished them good luck with everything, and Mary and Jesse went to the lobby to meet their friends who had come to take them in for as long as they needed a place to stay.

Angie watched them leave and had to stifle the urge to call them back.

19

Angie and Chief Martin entered the day room at the hospital where patients could meet with family and friends in a space other than their rooms. The large space was arranged into groups of sitting areas and the big windows allowed in lots of light to make a cheerful, pleasant gathering place.

The chief glanced around and spotted a woman waving at them who matched Roberta Reynolds's description. A young woman sat in a wheelchair next to her.

"Hello. I'm Roberta and this is Sally."

The two visitors took seats across from the women and introduced themselves.

"We spoke with your husband," the chief said. "He told us you both were doing well."

"Have you caught the guy yet?" Sally demanded. Her arm and leg were in casts and she had a patch over the eye that required surgery due to flying glass.

"We're still investigating," the chief gave the young woman a reassuring nod and then turned his gaze to the mother. "Would you be able to describe the day of the explosion for us?"

Roberta winced slightly at the word *explosion*, but she shook it off and forced a smile. "I'd be glad to, especially if what we have to say will lead to the person responsible." Taking a deep breath, she spoke about the day. "I took the day off from work so Sally and I could spend some time together before school started up again. We had lunch at home, made some cookies, and decided to watch a movie together. Sally suggested we make a fire in the fireplace for a cozy atmosphere. She went out to the wood pile and brought in a bucket of logs. We set them up, I lit them, and we sat down on the sofa. They didn't catch very well so Sally went over to move them around with the poker. We were a few minutes into the movie when it happened."

Roberta clasped her hands together and her

breathing rate seemed to increase. "I remember the awful noise. I honestly don't remember anything else until I woke up here in the hospital."

Angie turned to Sally. "Is that how you remember the day?"

"Pretty much." The young woman was looking down at the floor.

"In retrospect, when you were out at the wood pile, did anything look unusual or off in any way?" Angie asked.

"Unusual how?"

"I don't know. Did the pile look like it always did? Were some of the logs arranged in a different way?"

"I didn't notice anything," Sally said.

"You collected the logs and bought them inside?"

"Right."

"What happened when you brought them in?" the chief asked.

Sally gave him a look like he was stupid. "They exploded."

"Right away?" The chief wanted to hear Sally's recollection.

"No, we were watching the movie like my mom said, then all of a sudden the room lit up and there was a terrible noise. The window blew out I think.

Glass flew in every direction. I went up in the air and them smashed to the floor. It all happened in a split second. I remember being on my back on the floor. I couldn't hear anything. I couldn't see much. I didn't feel hurt even though I was injured. There wasn't any pain. I almost felt like I was floating, looking down on the family room from way up high." Sally paused for a few seconds. "That's it. That's all I remember."

"You've been to the house?" Roberta asked.

"We were there to speak with your husband," Angie said.

"How does the house look?" Roberta looked to Angie. "Is it a terrible mess? Is the family room damaged beyond repair? I ask Lincoln about it, but he brushes off my questions."

"The family room had damage done to it. Some windows were broken, some of the ceiling came down, some stones in the fireplace broke apart and fell off," Angie listed the things she'd noticed when she was there. "Your husband is having it renovated and repaired. It's in progress right now."

Roberta nodded her head. "I think Lincoln wants the room to be perfect when we get home. He doesn't want any reminders of the explosion." With a sigh, she said, "We'd just had the whole house refreshed. All the rooms were painted, new furniture was purchased and delivered. It had all been done for only a week, and then the family room was ruined. I'm sure it will be nice again soon."

Angie perked up from what Roberta had said. "You had the house redone?"

"Just paint and new furniture. It needed an update."

"Did you hire people to paint?"

"Sure. Lincoln and I don't have the time to do a project like that on our own. It would take forever if we tried to do it ourselves. We hired a company to do the painting of the rooms and we hired a designer to help us with the furniture."

"What company did you hire for the painting?" Angie asked.

"Blue Sky. They do good work."

"Except when the painters make you angry," Sally piped up.

"They made you angry?" Angie asked.

Roberta put a hand on her ribs and adjusted her position in her chair. "Some of the men on the team didn't get along. Two of them actually. One was always picking at the other one, and there were times when the picked-on one blew up. They had words, hurled insults and curses at each other. I'd had enough. I told them to stop it, to stop acting like children. I didn't want their mutual antagonism to influence the quality of the painting work. I felt like they were spending more time picking at each other than getting the work done, the work we were paying for. I lit into them one day. I told them not to come back if they couldn't control themselves. I spoke to the owner about them. We didn't want those two creating an atmosphere of discord in our home."

Angie knew who Roberta was talking about. "How did the men take your criticism?"

"Not well. One of them stormed out. He told me to do it myself. Can you imagine?"

"How about the other man?"

Robert said, "He looked angry, but he didn't say much. He went back to work. The other one never came back. I assume the owner assigned the one who stormed out to another team. We didn't get anyone to replace him so the project took longer than it was supposed to. I can't blame the company. The employees have to behave professionally. Unfortunately, some workers don't understand the kind of behavior that's expected."

"Did the painters go in and out of the house

through the front or back doors?" Chief Martin asked.

"The back. They came in through the French doors in the kitchen," Roberta said.

"Do you know the names of the men who were arguing with each other?"

"Dave? I don't recall the other man's name. Dave was hard to talk to, he seemed shy or annoyed, I could never tell which one it was. He didn't seem to mingle with the others. At lunchtime, Dave would go for a walk. He never ate with the other painters."

"You stayed at home during the painting?" Angie asked.

"Lincoln and I had to take time off from work to stay home. We didn't want people in the house without one of us around. We wanted to keep an eye on the workers. I didn't want them free to wander wherever they felt like going."

"Do either of you know the other targeted people?" Chief Martin asked.

Roberta and Sally exchanged looks.

"We don't know them," Roberta said. "We never crossed paths with any of them."

Sally shook her head.

"Did you have any issues with any of your friends recently?" the chief asked Sally.

"No, no issues."

"How about with your patients or colleagues? Were there any disagreements or disgruntled clients?"

"Nothing was wrong," Roberta said. "There weren't any problems at work. Everything was fine."

20

ngie, Courtney, and Chief Martin sat in the living room of Dennis and Carol Leeds's house. In her forties, Carol was short and trim and had chin-length blond hair and blue eyes. Her manner was friendly and open and when the two sisters and the chief arrived, she'd made them drinks and put out a platter of cheese, crackers, and nuts.

The chief's friend, Solana's Chief of Police Benny Peterson, asked them to visit with the Leeds's to answer some of the couple's questions and to see if they had anything new to say.

Angie felt like a bundle of nerves, but had no reason for her unease. She'd talked with Dennis before and thought he was honest and forthcoming so there was no reason to feel antsy about the visit.

"Is there anything new with the case?" Dennis asked.

"The leads are being investigated." The chief tried to reassure the man who found the package bomb in his mailbox.

"It seems like a lot of time has passed and nothing has come out of it. No one has been arrested. Are we supposed to live in fear for the rest of our lives?" Dennis was testy about what he perceived as slow progress in finding the bomber.

"Investigations take time," the chief told the man. "It may seem like nothing is happening, but I assure you the case has the utmost priority. It appears that a lot of time has passed, but it's only been about ten days."

Dennis blew out a breath. "We'd just like it solved. Get the freak behind bars so we can stop worrying about every little noise we hear."

"Has anything new come to mind since we last spoke?" Angie asked. "Any little thing you might have remembered that might be helpful?"

Dennis's shoulders slumped. "I think about it all the time. What if I had handled the package? What if I hadn't come home early that day and Carol picked up the mail? One of us could have been killed. It's a very sobering thought." Dennis had dark circles under his eyes and the wrinkles around his mouth looked deeper. Angie thought he must be having trouble sleeping.

"Have you thought back over the days and weeks prior to receiving the package in your mailbox? Does anything stand out that might point to someone who was angry with you?" Courtney had taken the chief's example and had a small notebook in her lap where she was writing a few notes.

"Nothing. I haven't had any issues with anyone." Dennis looked to his wife.

"I haven't either," Carol said.

"What about the guy across the street?" Dennis brought up Dave Hanes. "He was watching me when I was getting the mail. He was in his driveway. I saw him out of the corner of my eye."

"There's nothing that points to Dave Hanes," the chief said.

"Did you talk to him?" Dennis wanted to know.

Chief Martin nodded. "We did. Several times. So have the detectives on the case, as well as Chief Peterson and his officers."

Dennis rolled his eyes. "I don't trust him. Don't take him off your list of suspects."

"Why don't you trust him?" Courtney asked.

"He seems odd. Can never stop what he's doing to talk to the neighbors."

"He might be shy," Courtney said. "He might feel that he won't know what to say. He inherited the house from his parents. It might take him time to feel comfortable in the neighborhood."

"Sheesh," Dennis said. "He's been living here for at least six months. How much time does he need to feel comfortable?"

"Everyone is different," Angie explained. "Everyone has different fears and worries and insecurities."

Carol agreed. "Some people take longer than others to settle in. Maybe the neighbor has always had low self-esteem and feels awkward around others. It's no reason to suspect him."

Dennis sighed. "I don't care who the culprit is. I only want him found, tried, and convicted. Then I can rest easy again."

"That is law enforcement's goal as well," Chief Martin said.

Courtney asked, "Was there anyone who recently lived in the neighborhood who got into disagreements with the other people who lived here?"

Dennis was about to shake his head, but

thought of something. "There was a guy who lived around the block with his girlfriend. He was big, not heavy, but muscular. He didn't seem to work, was always around during the day. He didn't seem to do much. The girlfriend worked and she did everything outside, too. She mowed the lawn, painted the fence, shoveled in the winter. Anyway, the guy was always having disputes with his neighbors. One family put one of those basketball hoop stands at the end of the cul-de-sac and this guy told them they had to take it down. He started an argument with the neighbor on one side saying their fence was too far over into the girlfriend's yard. All kinds of stuff like that. He was a troublemaker. A day didn't go by when he wasn't all up in arms about some crime someone had committed down that way. The people on that street couldn't stand him. They were happy when he moved away."

"Do you know his name?" Courtney asked.

"Tom. I don't know if I ever heard the last name. I can find out for you."

"Do you know where Tom moved to?" Chief Martin asked.

Dennis rubbed his chin. "Let's see. Revere? I can find out the details if you want. The girlfriend still lives here. I heard she got sick of him and she kicked the guy out."

After another twenty minutes of discussion, the meeting drew to a close and the investigators left the house. The chief was heading back to the center of Sweet Cove and offered to drop Courtney back at the Victorian. Angie had borrowed Jenna's car and was heading to the museum bake shop so they decided to get-together later with the chief to go over some of the details of the case.

As Courtney and the chief drove away, Angie was about to get into her car when Carol Leeds came out of the house and called to her.

"Do you have a few more minutes?" Carol asked while she looked back to her front door.

"Sure. Shall I come back in?" Angie asked.

"Um. Do you mind if we sit in your car?"

A shiver of nervousness slipped over Angie's skin. "Okay. We can do that."

When the women were settled in the front seats, Carol said, "Dennis is working in his office. If we talked inside, he'd hear us. I'd rather talk privately."

Angie nodded.

"Dennis is having a hard time with what happened. He can't sleep, he rants about the bomber, he's anxious and moody. I suggested he see the doctor, but he keeps putting it off."

"Would you like one of us to speak with him?"

"Oh, no." Carol blinked. "That isn't what I want to talk about." The woman looked to her house to be sure Dennis wasn't coming out. "I work as an emergency room nurse at the hospital in Sweet Cove. I've been there almost twenty years."

Angie searched Carol's face. "Did something happen when you were at work?"

"One evening, I was working the late shift. I don't usually, but a friend asked if I could cover for her and we switched shifts that day. A guy came in. He'd been stabbed. It wasn't bad, the wound was on the upper arm near the shoulder. He needed stitches. I described his injury and explained the need to have it stitched. Well, he became so angry. He called me names, said I didn't know anything, that I was trying to hurt him. He was irrational. He grabbed for my neck, but I was able to twist away from his grasp." Carol paused and ran her hand across her forehead. "Anyway, an officer came in with a few of the doctors. They'd heard the commotion and rushed to my aid. I left and didn't go back to the room."

"Did he leave the hospital without getting the care he needed?' Angie asked.

"He did. I was coming out of another treatment room and almost ran into him. He was leaving. When he saw me, his face got all distorted with anger. He leaned down and whispered, "Carol Leeds. Watch your back. I'll find out where you live."

A cold shiver ran down Angie's back.

"You think this man might be the bomber? When did this happen?"

"It happened about a month ago. I don't know if this man is responsible for leaving that package bomb in our mailbox, but you asked if Dennis or I experienced any problems with someone so I thought I should tell you. I haven't told Dennis. I knew he'd be furious that the guy had done this. And I don't want to tell him now because he's been so upset by the bombs."

"Can you tell me the man's name?" Angie's heart raced.

"I can't." Carol shook her head. "I could lose my job if I told you. There are regulations regarding patient privacy. But I thought if I told you about the incident, you could tell Chief Martin or Chief Peterson and they could speak with the hospital administrators. The administrators might be able to tell law enforcement the man's name."

"Good idea," Angie said. "I'll pass the information on to Chief Martin."

"I don't want Dennis to get wind of this. Chief Martin won't ask him anything about it, will he? Dennis is upset enough already."

"I'll tell the chief that you want to keep Dennis from hearing about it, but at some point, you'll probably need to tell him."

"I know." Carol glanced at the house. "He's taking all of this so hard. I'm afraid for his health. Why did any of this have to happen?" Some tears gathered at the corners of her eyes and one rolled down the woman's cheek.

Angie's mind was in a whirl and she realized that this was the reason she was so nervous when she arrived at the Leeds's house. She was able to sense Carol's worry.

The man at the hospital could very well be the bomber, and he must have targeted Carol.

21

Tom, Mr. Finch, the four sisters, and the two cats gathered in the backyard to go over some plans for changes to the carriage house. Tom, with Euclid and Circe strolling behind him, walked the future periphery of the carriage house to show the new footprint.

"The addition would go straight off this way, then like this. I can put stakes in the ground to give you a better idea of what it would look like." Tom handed Jenna a measuring tape and they created the invisible addition by measuring the length of the sides and hammering the stakes into place. The cats sat in the middle of it.

"What do you two think?" Tom asked the felines.

Euclid and Circe trilled.

"It doesn't take up much of the yard," Finch observed.

"And the way you've positioned it," Angie said, "the big tree doesn't have to come down."

Ellie held an architect's sketch of the carriage house showing the addition. "It's a smart design. It gives Mr. Finch a first-floor two-bedroom apartment and there'll be an additional two-bedroom apartment on the second floor that can be rented out."

"It's the most bang for the buck," Tom told them.

"I like it." Courtney stepped inside the area that would become the addition and walked around imagining the layout. She turned to Finch and smiled. "Come in here, Mr. Finch, and see how you like it."

Finch obliged the young woman, and Courtney held his hand as she showed him his new apartment.

"Here's the front door." Ellie pointed out where it would go. "You walk straight into your living room. There's a gas fireplace on the left wall."

Courtney and Finch moved about the space at Ellie's direction pretending to see everything she described.

"The kitchen and dining space is open to the

living room. There's a hall on the right that leads to the bathroom and the two bedrooms."

"It's beautiful, Mr. Finch. I think you'll be very happy here." Courtney smiled.

Ellie looked again at the plans and sketches. "There's also an optional sunroom off the kitchen."

The cats trilled when they heard about the sunroom.

"Oh," Courtney's voice was excited. "You should definitely go for the sunroom. You can set up your art desk in there. There'll be great light for drawing and painting."

"We can do the other option, too," Tom said. "We can make a larger apartment in the carriage house, but it would be on the second floor."

Finch glanced around at the stakes in the ground and didn't speak for a few moments. He brushed at his eyes and turned around. "Are you sure you want to add on to the carriage house?" he asked the sisters.

"We'll do whatever suits you," Ellie told the man. "It's your choice."

"There's another option we haven't discussed." Tom removed some papers from his back pocket and unrolled them. "We could also add on to the Victorian at the back of the house." As Tom strode across the lawn to the rear of the mansion, the cats raced ahead. "We could make the addition right here off the family room. It would be similar to the addition off the carriage house, but it would be a little bigger. The other nice feature is that you would have direct access to the house. You wouldn't have to go outside in the rain or snow. There'd be no chance of slipping on the ice when you leave your place and go into the main house."

Courtney whooped. "What a fabulous idea. Your apartment will be right off the family room. It would be so convenient, especially when you're watching the babies."

"We'd have to move the patio and the pergola a little further back, but that's no big deal," Tom said. "It's a very large yard. The space won't be missed if we use some of it for the addition." He handed the design sheet to Mr. Finch and when the older man was done examining it, he passed it to Courtney, and it went around the group so everyone could take a look.

"What do you think, Mr. Finch?" Courtney asked him.

Finch's lower lip trembled slightly. "I think it's perfect." He looked to the sisters. "Would you be okay with adding directly onto the house?"

The sisters all spoke at the same time, saying the same things.

"It's the best choice. It would be wonderful to have your place attached to the main house. A first floor apartment will be helpful as you get older and we'll only be steps away from you."

As Finch was surrounded by hugs, the gentle man brushed at his eyes. "I am truly blessed."

Angie, Courtney, and Mr. Finch went into the kitchen while Tom left to go to a renovation site, Jenna returned to the jewelry shop, and Ellie tended to some B and B guests.

As Angie put on water for tea and Finch took three cups from the cabinet, Courtney brought a notebook over to the kitchen table.

"I've made a spreadsheet and a map." She removed a large piece of paper from the notebook and spread it over the tabletop. "I know the police are doing this, but I wanted to do it, too, so I could visualize the details."

Euclid and Circe listened from the top of the refrigerator.

"What is it, Miss Courtney?" Finch adjusted his glasses.

"The map shows the places in Solana Village where the package bombs were placed. I was looking for a pattern or some connection between the locations. See? The red triangles indicate the places where the victims are located."

Finch and Angie gazed at the map.

"Were you able to discover any links between the sites?" Finch asked.

"No. If we go by location alone, there doesn't seem to be a pattern or a connection," Courtney told them. "I also made this spread sheet that lists the victims, their addresses, the family members, their occupations and places of employment, clubs or groups they belong to, and miscellaneous details that don't fit into any particular category."

Angie stared at her sister. "This is impressive."

"I decided we can't just rely on our paranormal skills to solve this thing. I'm sort of obsessed with finding the bomber so I'm employing all of my abilities to flush him out."

"Have you arrived at any conclusions?" Finch asked.

"Not yet." Courtney made eye contact with her sister and Finch. "But my sense is that the victims have met the bomber. They know him ... maybe only in passing, but they know who he is."

The little blond hairs on Angie's arms stood up. "You gathered that from the spreadsheet?"

"Not really. The feeling bubbled up while I was working on it. I'm sure the bomber is familiar to each of the victims. That fact may as well be written on the spreadsheet because I know it's true."

"You're right." Angie felt a surge of adrenaline rush through her veins. She knew that Courtney was correct. "How could each of the victims know the bomber? Do they all frequent the same establishment like a grocery store, gas station, or coffee shop?"

"That hasn't been established yet," Courtney sighed.

"You're on the right track," Finch nodded. "I can feel it. Miss Ellie believes the acts of violence are not random. She is sure the victims have been chosen for a reason. Her theory lines up with your idea that the victims know their attacker."

Angie hadn't had a chance to tell the family what she'd learned from Carol Leeds about the episode at the hospital where an injured man had made a threat towards the woman so she reported it to Courtney and Finch.

"Could the hospital be the place where the bomber met his victims?" Angie offered. "We should ask Chief Martin to find out if any of the package bomb victims were at the hospital on the night this man was there for treatment."

"What about an auto body shop or car repair shop?" Finch questioned. "The victims all drive vehicles and they may have gone to the same garage for service. The bomber might be an employee there."

"Chief Martin told me he wants us to interview the young couple again whose car blew up," Angie said. "I'll bring up the repair shop idea with them and see where they usually brought their car for service."

"We need to find the connection between the victims," Courtney said. "I'm determined to figure this out." She took a sip of tea. "Can you bake something?" she asked her sister. "I could use something sweet to help me think."

"I have to go to the museum bake shop in a few minutes," Angie said. "But maybe I'll bake this evening. Baking always clears my head. What would you like me to make?"

"Something chocolate. Maybe with some strawberries. Surprise me."

"I'll come up with something," Angie smiled.

Courtney said, "If you need us, Mr. Finch and I will be at the candy store until closing tonight. We have a lot of online orders to get out and one of the employees is sick. Come by later. Bring Ellie and Jenna if they're are available. We can have a family pow-wow."

Euclid meowed from his perch on the fridge.

With a nod to the big orange boy, Courtney added, "Bring the cats, too."

Because the day was sunny with comfortable temperatures, Angie decided to walk to the museum bake shop to get some fresh air and exercise, but with each step she took, her anxiety level increased. She was so apprehensive, that every few minutes, she glanced over her shoulder and looked at the passing tourists with suspicion.

Chiding herself for being such a worrier, Angie turned the corner to the museum and saw a woman sitting on one of the granite benches outside.

Mary Foley, the woman whose car had blown up, stood and waved at Angie. "One of the bake shop employees told me you'd be in soon. Do you have a few minutes to talk?"

Is this the reason I was so on edge while walking down here?

22

After Angie spoke with her employees, she carried two cups of tea to the small café table in the three-story, light-filled atrium where she and Mary took seats.

"Sorry to bother you at work." Mary's face had a heavy look.

"No bother. It's not busy right now. How can I help?"

Mary's fingers trembled when she reached for her cup. "You were nice when you all came to talk with me and Jesse. I wanted to talk to you again. That was just about the worst day of our lives. It was so incredible to think someone tried to kill us. I can't wrap my head around that. What did we do to instigate such a reaction? How can someone make an attempt on another person's life over nothing? I've been wrestling with these thoughts since the car blew up." Mary took in a deep breath. "Every time I say those words, I shudder inside."

"It's understandable. It was an awful shock." Angie waited to hear the reason Mary wanted to speak with her. "How is Jesse doing?"

"You think you can handle bad things ... until bad things happen and you find yourself struggling to cope." Mary absentmindedly pushed her auburn hair back from her shoulder. "Jesse and I get depressed sometimes, and once in a while we snip at each other. We both know it comes from dealing with feelings about the attack, but it makes us feel badly that there are times when we aren't kind to each other. We're going to see a counselor for some help handling our feelings. We've lost our sense of safety. We both feel very vulnerable."

"It's a good idea to talk with someone," Angie praised the couple's decision.

"We might not rebuild," Mary said. "I think we'd rather leave and buy somewhere else. Neither one of us wants to stay where there are such bad memories. It would be a constant reminder that we could have been killed that night."

"I might feel the same way." Angie wasn't sure

how she would react in Jesse and Mary's situation. She and her sisters had managed to escape a fire in the carriage house that was set with the intention to murder them, but maybe the episode didn't take a heavy toll on them emotionally because they'd managed to escape the blaze. Jesse and Mary's situation had depended a lot on luck and Angie thought that would be harder to rationalize when chance alone played the major role in your survival.

Mary took another sip from her cup and glanced around. "This is a beautiful museum. Jesse and I love to come here. Your bakery is a great addition."

Angie thanked the young woman for her compliment. "Does Jesse know you're talking to me?"

Mary's eyes flicked down at her cup and then back up to Angie. "I didn't tell him."

"Why not?"

"I want to tell you about something that happened not too long ago. If you think it's important, then I'll talk to Chief Peterson and Chief Martin. I wanted your input first. I'm not sure if I'm being concerned over nothing."

"What happened?" Angie felt a flutter of unease.

Mary began her story. "Jesse and I went out for dinner at the Irish pub in Silver Cove. They have live music some nights."

"I know the place." Angie nodded.

"We had great meals and we decided to stay for drinks to listen to the music."

When Mary didn't go on, Angie asked, "Did something happen?"

"Yes," Mary's voice was soft. "We went out to the parking lot. Some guy had blocked us in with his truck. He was sitting in it so we went over and asked if he could move so we could leave. The man got really angry, swore at us. I told him we wanted to go home and when we left the parking space he'd be able to take it. Well, he jumped out of the truck like a wild man. I got so scared. Jesse told him we didn't want any trouble, that we'd like to go home."

Mary gulped down the last of her tea and went on with the tale. "The guy smelled like alcohol. He took a swing at Jesse, but Jesse sidestepped him. That seemed to infuriate the man. Jesse told me to get in the car, count to ten, and then lean on the horn. While I hurried to our car, Jesse tried to reason with the man, but the guy was having a fit. I counted to ten and then hit the horn. It was a little diversion that gave Jesse the chance to run to the car and jump in. He started the engine and hit the gas. We were parked facing the sidewalk. The car flew over the sidewalk, bumped over the curb, and off we went down the street. Guess what happened next?"

A hard cold ball of dread had settled in Angie's stomach. "He came after you."

"Yes. We didn't know he was following us. He kept back a few cars behind. When we turned into our neighborhood, Jesse noticed the truck. He was about to turn into our driveway, but instead sped up and drove away. The truck stopped in front of our house for a few minutes, then it backed up in our driveway and left the neighborhood the way we came in. We don't have a garage so we were afraid to go home and park in the driveway in case the man came back. We drove around for a while. After about twenty minutes, we went home."

"The man in the truck wasn't around?" Angie asked.

"He wasn't." Mary shook her head. "I was all shook up. Neither one of us slept a wink all night. I was waiting for that man to bang on our door, or to break in."

"Did you call the police?"

Mary swallowed hard. "We know now it was stupid not to. We just wanted the episode to go away. We worried that if we reported it, the police might reveal our names and the guy would come after us."

"Can you describe the man?"

Mary's shoulder slumped. "Not very well. It was so frightening you'd think we'd remember every detail, but we didn't. He was average height, a regular build. Not heavy, not slim. It was dark so I don't know the color of his eyes or his hair. He had on a baseball cap. The name of a business was embroidered over the pocket of his shirt."

Angie didn't need to hear the name to know what it said.

"It was Blue Sky Painting," Mary told her.

"Was the man's name embroidered on the shirt?"

"Just the business name."

"Can you describe the truck?"

"It was a dark color. I don't know what kind of truck it was. Jesse doesn't know either. The shock of the experience seems to have frozen our brains. Jesse likes cars and trucks and he usually remembers people's vehicles. He didn't that night."

"Was there anything else about the man that stood out?"

Mary shook her head.

"Can you remember what he was wearing?"

"Jeans? I don't know what he had on his feet."

"Did you, by any chance, get some of his license plate numbers?"

"No. I didn't think to do that. We were panicked. Our good sense deserted us when we needed it most."

Angie gave the woman a warm smile. "That's not true. Your good sense got you out of there and you acted appropriately when you saw the truck near your house. You protected yourselves. When an emergency happens, we often react like we're on autopilot. Your self-preservation instincts kicked in and you got yourselves out of harm's way. So, no, your good sense didn't desert you."

"Thanks, but in retrospect we should have reported the incident to the police."

"Do you think the person who planted the bomb in your car could be the guy who harassed you in the restaurant parking lot?"

"I think it's possible." Mary leaned closer. "Do you think so?"

"It's very possible. It's great that you noticed the business name on the man's shirt."

"We failed at getting a description of the guy though. Jesse and I were both embarrassed about how little we could recall about the man."

"It's not unusual. That happens very frequently."

"Should I tell the police about that night?" Mary

asked cautiously. "I don't want them to think I'm overreacting."

"I think you should definitely tell them. It could be a very important clue to solving the case." Angie's mind was racing. It could have been anyone who worked for Blue Sky Painting, but she had two suspects in mind. Dave Hanes and Joe Boles. Both had reputations for being easy to anger. Dave Hanes had a truck. Angie had seen it in his driveway. Was the man who tormented Jesse and Mary the bomber? It was a stretch to think so, but the possibility had to be investigated.

The Reynolds family had employed Blue Sky Painting and both Dave and Joe worked on their home before the men were split up to different teams. They'd been caught arguing by the homeowners. One of the men might have seen the wood pile. One of them could be the bomber.

But what about Carol and Dennis Leeds? What connection could they have had to the painting company. Did they have work done on their house? Angie made a mental note to find out.

And then there was Agnes Shield, the first victim. Had the Shields' employed the painters? Did they update the paint inside or outside the house? Angie thought hard about the condition of the home, but couldn't recall if it looked freshly painted. Is this idea just a wild goose chase? Are we going down the wrong path? What were they missing? She needed to talk to Chief Martin.

"Angie?" Mary spoke.

Angie blinked a few times. "Oh, sorry. My mind is going over what you told me. What did you ask?"

"How will you find out who the man in the truck is?"

"The police will look into it," Angie assured the young woman. "The police will figure it out."

She hoped.

23

ourtney picked up Angie outside the museum. "What's cookin'?"

"Plenty." Angie told her sister where to drive to.

Courtney pulled away from the curb. "Why there?"

"We need to talk to the owner." Angie reported what Mary Foley told her about the man in the truck acting irrational and harassing her and her husband one night outside a restaurant.

"Wow. This could be the break we need," Courtney said. "The guy in the truck sounds like he's got quite a few issues. He's dangerous. He shouldn't be allowed to drive. They should take his license away."

"Mary and Jesse's experience in the restaurant parking lot may have nothing to do with the bomber, but it needs to be checked out."

"Did you tell Chief Martin?"

"I called him. He's going to call the owner of Blue Sky Painting to tell him we're coming, but the chief can't leave the station right now. That's why he asked if we'd go over and talk to the owner face to face." Angie watched the landscape go by as the car moved down the road. "Something's been going through my mind since I heard Mary's story."

Courtney gave her sister a quick look. "What is it? Do you have an idea?"

"Dennis Leeds is the only victim whose bomb didn't go off."

Stopping at a red light, Courtney turned to Angie. "You think Dennis Leeds is the bomber?"

"I don't know. I've been wondering about the circumstances. Dennis went out to get the mail, he noticed the package, but didn't touch it. He went back in the house, but didn't call the police. His wife came home and when she heard there was an unexpected package in their mailbox, she notified the police. Why didn't Dennis report the package when he saw it?"

The light turned green and Courtney accelerated. "Dennis might have wanted his wife's opinion. He might not want to seem like an alarmist. Maybe he wanted to talk it over with Carol before he did anything."

"That could be." Angie sighed. "Dennis is always telling us how odd his neighbor is. He's often pointed his finger at Dave Hanes to make us suspicious of him."

"It could be that Dennis *is* suspicious of Dave."

Angie said, "Dennis could also be making a big deal of the man's shyness and withdrawn manner to take suspicion off *himself*."

"It's possible. So you're thinking Dennis may have planted bombs at Agnes Shield's house, at the Reynolds family's house, and in Mary and Jesse Foley's car? Why though?"

"I don't have an answer for his motivation," Angie said. "He's a plumber. Maybe he worked at their houses and became angry with them for some reason. He decided he'd had enough and wanted them dead." She lifted her hands in a helpless gesture. "Or maybe he's got issues, and there's no reason at all and he chose his victims at random."

"Dennis's wife, Carol, told you about a man at the hospital who threatened her," Courtney reminded her sister. "Do you think that man has nothing to do with the bombs now?"

"I don't know," Angie said. "Chief Martin and Chief Peterson are asking the hospital administrators for the name of the man who caused the trouble. If they get the name, they can investigate him. I'm coming up with suspects based on what we know right now. When new information comes in, I'll adjust my thinking."

"I think you have a good idea about Dennis Leeds. He can't be ruled out." Courtney nodded as she pulled into the Blue Sky Painting Company's parking lot. "The other suspects are the man in the truck who harassed the Foley's and the man at the hospital who threatened Carol Leeds. Who else? Are you putting Dave Hanes on the list?"

"Yes. He was one of the painters working at the Reynolds's house. He might have seen the wood pile and got the notion to hide a bomb in it."

"What about the guy Dave fought with, Joe Boles?" Courtney asked. "He sounds like trouble."

"I agree. He should be on the suspect list. He was painting at the Reynolds's house, too." Angie glanced at the front door to Blue Sky. "But what connection do these men have to the other victims?"

"Let's go talk to the owner. Maybe we'll learn something new."

The sisters got out of the car and entered the office to meet with Bruce Brown.

"Nice to see you again." Bruce shook hands with Angie and Courtney, and ushered them into his small office. "Chief Martin spoke with me by phone a little while ago. I have to tell you I'm very upset by this. Someone from my company is going around tormenting people? I need to know who did that. I won't have someone like that associated with the company. I don't care if alcohol is to blame. It's not an excuse for such behavior."

"From what the chief told you, do you have an idea who this might be?" Angie asked.

"I might have, but I can't accuse anyone until I know more," Bruce told them.

"Have Dave Hanes or Joe Boles caused any more trouble at work?" Courtney questioned.

Bruce leaned back in his chair and let out a long sigh. "Since you're working with the police, I'll tell you. I fired both of them yesterday."

Angie sat up. "You did? Why?"

Rubbing the back of his neck, Bruce told them the reasons. "There's an employee room in here. Most guys come by in the morning before they head off to their assignments for the day. They have coffee, get their assignments, talk with the other guys, pick up equipment, and head out. Yesterday morning, Dave and Joe had another altercation. They were yelling, arguing, and then Joe punched Dave and a fist-fight broke out. Those two can't control themselves when they're together. It was a toxic situation that threatened to infect the other employees so I had to end it. They're both skilled workers, but that doesn't matter if they're going to wreak havoc here at work."

"How did they handle being let go?" A tingle of worry nagged at Angie.

"Dave listened to my reasoning, then he nodded, accepted the paperwork, got up and left. He didn't say a word. I felt bad about it. The way he took it, made me feel worse."

"And Joe Boles?" Courtney asked. "How did he take it?"

"Not as well. At least, not as quietly." Bruce shook his head. "He ranted at me, told me it was all Dave's fault. He said Dave was always the instigator. Dave was quiet so nobody noticed how he needled Joe. Honestly? I don't believe a single word of it. Joe had it in for Dave. He couldn't stand Dave staying to himself, acting shy, being so introverted. I don't know way it bothered Joe so much, but that's what it was like. I couldn't let one go and not the other. They both have blame in the game."

"Did Joe calm down and leave?"

"He didn't really calm down." Bruce looked stressed recalling the morning. "I told him his yelling was unacceptable and that he'd have to leave. I told him to write me an email outlining his complaints. I told him to email a copy to the state department of labor and file a complaint against me. Joe got a gleam in his eye when he heard that. He cursed at me a few more times, and then he stormed out."

"Chief Martin told you that Mary Foley reported that a man in a restaurant parking lot who harassed them and followed them home was wearing a shirt from your company. If the man didn't work here, how could someone get hold of a company shirt?" Angie questioned.

Bruce shrugged. "I guess it could be someone who used to work here. Or maybe one of my employees lent a brother or a friend a shirt? We gave some away at a 10k race we sponsored last spring, but those were t-shirts. Was the shirt the guy had on a polo or a t-shirt?"

"I don't know. We can find out." Courtney wrote a reminder in her notebook.

"Do you know Dennis Leeds?" Angie asked. "He's a plumber who lives in town."

"I don't think so." Bruce shook his head, but stopped. "Wait, wasn't he one of the bomber's victims?"

"He found the package in his mailbox, but he didn't pick it up. Do you have a list of the people who entered the 10k race?"

"I don't. The race organizer would have that. I believe they keep the information on file," Bruce told Angie. "I can give you the name of the organizer."

Angie thanked him. "Do you have any concerns that Dave Hanes or Joe Boles will retaliate against you for letting them go?"

Bruce frowned. "I didn't … until you just brought it up."

"Do you think either one of the men is capable of doing something in anger because he was fired?" Courtney asked.

"I suppose so. The way they behaved towards each other is a red flag, I guess. I never gave it any thought." Bruce shifted uncomfortably in his seat.

"Do you think I'd better watch out? Do you think I should be on guard?"

"I don't think it would hurt to be watchful," Angie chose her words carefully.

"Great." Bruce ran his hand over his face. "As if I don't have enough on my mind, now I have to watch my back in case one of those guys has to act out his anger." His eyes widened and he stared at the sisters. "You aren't thinking that Dave or Joe could actually be the bomber, are you?"

"We just gather information for the police," Courtney fibbed a little. "We really don't know who the police suspect."

24

Euclid and Circe watched from the top of the refrigerator while Angie mixed the ingredients for a chocolate pie. The details of the case ran through her mind as she worked. So much of her and the family's suspicions revolved around speculation and not much in the way of concrete facts.

They needed more information. Chief Martin and Chief Peterson were still negotiating with the hospital for the name of the man who threatened Carol Leeds, and Chief Martin had requested the names of the participants of Solana's spring 10k road race since shirts with Blue Sky Painting on them had been given out that day to the runners.

But where are the connections between the victims?

Angie knew that Dave Hanes and Joe Boles had been working at the Reynolds's house, but Dennis and Carol Leeds hadn't had any painting done at their home. Agnes Shield's husband told the police they hadn't hired anyone to paint and neither had Jesse and Mary Foley.

Dave and Joe could only be linked to the Reynolds's household.

Looking off into space, Angie rested her whisk on a small plate. How would the case be solved? How would they find the clues they needed? She hoped it wouldn't be because the bomber got care-less and left a clue when he targeted more people.

It has to stop before someone gets killed.

Angie spotted Courtney's case spreadsheets and notes on the kitchen table and went over to look at them again. Thankfully, there were no new markers on the map indicating new victims. Angie reviewed the list of names, family members, addresses, and jobs Courtney had compiled. Her eyes moved from the map to the spreadsheet. And then, she noticed something in the spreadsheet notes she'd forgotten.

Agnes's husband, Everett, mentioned that Agnes had been yelled at by a painter who was working across the street.

It must have been the same painter who had been rude to her and Jenna when they parked near the house momentarily. It must have been Joe Boles. The company doing the work nearby was Blue Sky.

Angie looked up and stared across the room at nothing.

Joe Boles and Dave Hanes were working across the street from the Shield's house. Joe or Dave, if one of them was the bomber, may have chosen Agnes as a victim while working in the neighborhood.

Blue Sky might have connections to *two* of the victims. Could the company somehow have links to all of the victims?

Angie looked around the kitchen for Mr. Finch's sketchbook, and then she remembered her sister had moved it to the sunroom desk. Before Angie went to look at it, she checked the time. Chief Martin had asked her and Jenna to meet him at Dave Hanes's house for a short meeting, and Jenna would be by soon to pick her up.

Slipping some wrap over the bowl of batter, she put it into the refrigerator to bake later, and then she hurried to the sunroom with the cats racing after her.

Sitting in one of the easy chairs by the big windows, Angie steeled herself to look at Mr. Finch's drawings. With each turn of a page, she became more anxious. Her heart pounded and her palms became sweaty.

Leaning closer, Angie realized what the pictures were trying to tell them all along. In each of the drawings, someone was standing on a ladder painting a building.

A painter.

That was the clue. All this time, the pictures were pointing them to a painter.

Euclid and Circe sat at attention on the rug looking up at Angie.

"The bomber is a painter," she told the cats.

Euclid let out a loud hiss, and Circe swished her tail back and forth.

"The bomber is either Joe Boles or Dave Hanes."

Angie heard the front door open and Jenna call to her. "Angie? Are you ready to go?"

～

WHILE JENNA DROVE, Angie chattered away about what she'd figured out.

"So you think it's Dave or Joe?" Jenna asked. "How can you tie them to the other victims?"

"I can't. Yet. But I know one of the painters is the bomber, and I know the bomber can be tied to everyone who has been targeted. We just need to figure out how. Maybe interviewing Dave today will give us the information we need."

"Why does Chief Martin want to talk to him again?" Jenna asked.

Angie's voice was excited. "I bet the chief and the other officers have a hunch Dave is the bomber, or they think he knows who the bomber is. Today's the day we're going to get answers. I can feel it."

"What about Dennis Leeds?" Jenna asked.

Angie deflated. "I was so sure one of the painters is the bomber, I forgot about Dennis." Letting out a moan, she said, "Lots of things point to Dennis as a suspect."

"True. But Mr. Finch's drawings seem to suggest a painter."

"They do." Angie perked up. "Let's see how the interview goes. I bet we're going to learn something important." Turning to her sister, she asked, "Do you have feelings one way or the other?"

It took a few moments for Jenna to reply. "The closer we get to Dave Hanes's house, the more nervous I feel."

"Is it because I was telling you he's a probable suspect?" Angie's concern was growing.

"I don't think it has anything to do with what you said. I've been on edge about this meeting all day."

Angie's heart dropped into her stomach as Jenna pulled the car to the curb in front of Dave's house.

"I don't see Chief Martin's car." Jenna cut the engine.

"He'll be here soon." Angie opened the door to get out. "Or maybe he got dropped off here by one of the officers." She checked her phone for messages, but there was nothing from the chief.

Dave came out of the garage and walked over to them when he saw the sisters standing by their car. "Chief Martin isn't here yet. Do you know why he wants to talk to me again?" He hadn't even bothered to say hello to the young women.

"I think he just wants to go over a few things," Angie said.

"What things?" Dave demanded.

"I really don't know. Chief Martin asked us to come. He didn't give us any details."

"I got fired." Dave's face was sad and drawn.

Angie and Jenna pretended they hadn't heard that Dave had lost his job.

"Did you?" Angie asked. "I'm sorry to hear that. What happened?"

"It was that Joe Boles. He caused it. He's always picking at me, making fun of me, saying rude things to make me feel bad."

"Did Joe start some trouble?" Jenna questioned.

"He was *always* starting trouble." Dave's voice was loud and angry.

"What happened this time?"

"He was making fun of me for being quiet. He swore at me, pushed me, pretended to strangle me. I can't stand him." Dave's hands had balled into fists.

"Maybe it will be better to work in a different place," Angie suggested. "Maybe it's good you won't have to see Joe anymore."

"It *will* be good, but I shouldn't have been fired. Joe was the only one who should have been let go. Not me. I was only defending myself against him."

"Could you talk to the owner once things have a chance to cool down?" Jenna asked. "Maybe you could tell him why you don't think you should have been fired."

"He should know that." Dave's face was bright red. "Why do I have to tell him?"

"It might help to talk to him," Jenna said. "It might help you get your job back."

Dave fumed for a few minutes. "Why doesn't the chief show up?"

"He'll be here soon."

"Do you want to come see the garden again? I'm overrun with tomatoes. Can I give you some vegetables to take home?"

Angie was surprised Dave had calmed down so quickly. "Sure. That would be nice."

"There are some baskets in the backyard," Dave told them. "You can fill them with any vegetables you want."

Following the man around the side of the house, little beads of nervous sweat started to trickle down Angie's back. She moved closer to Jenna and with every step she took, she felt more panicked.

"Maybe we should wait for Chief Martin," Angie said.

"Why?" Dave kept walking.

"He won't know where we are."

"He seems pretty smart. He'll see your car. I think he'll figure out that we're in the yard."

When they entered the rear yard, Dave pointed out which vegetables were where. "The lettuce is in the back. The carrots, beans, and cucumbers are over on that side. Tomatoes are on this side. There are baskets on the shelf by the door of the shed. Take whatever you want. Take some for the chief."

The sisters walked through the rows of vegetables towards the shed, but before they picked up the baskets, Angie, feeling more nervous by the second, looked around the yard and whispered to Jenna, "Let's go back to the car. We need to get out of here."

25

"Where are you going?" Dave looked surprised that the sisters were heading away from the shed.

"I'm feeling a little dizzy. I'm going to sit in the car for a few minutes." Angie touched her temple. It wasn't really a lie since her head truly was buzzing.

"The car will be hot. Come in and sit in the house. I'll get you some water." Dave stared as the sisters kept walking away. "Is something wrong?"

Angie's phone vibrated and she looked at the text. It was from the chief.

The hospital administrators gave us the name of the man who threatened Carol Leeds. It was Joe Boles. I'm on my way to Dave Hanes's house to meet you.

Jenna gasped just as Angie was looking up from her phone.

When Angie saw who had come around the corner to the backyard, her heart dropped into her stomach.

Joe Boles. Wearing a backpack. He halted steps from the sisters. "Is the cop here?"

"Chief Martin is on his way." Jenna tried to make her words sound forceful.

With an angry expression on his face, Dave hurried over to the three people and gave Joe an evil stare. "What are you doing here? You're trespassing. Get off my property."

"In a minute, I will. This won't take long." Joe grabbed Jenna by the arm.

"Let go of her," Angie demanded while trying to get hold of the man's arm, but Joe pushed her away.

Joe pulled a gun from the back of his waistband. "I could just go ahead and shoot the three of you, but I have a more fitting end." A wicked grin crossed his mouth and he shoved Jenna against her sister. "Give me your phones. Get in the shed. Move."

Dave started to shout obscenities at the man until Joe leveled the gun at him.

"Get going."

Angie, Jenna, and Dave trudged to the shed. Joe

pushed them inside, but not before leaving something on the floor. "Better not pick it up. Any little thing will set it off ... especially vibrations from anyone trying to break down the door. Don't worry though. It won't be long, then your worries will be over. See you." Joe gave them an ugly smile. "Or, maybe not." He closed the door softly.

They could hear the lock click into place.

"We're going to die." Dave clutched at his head, backed up against the wall of the twelve-foot by twelve-foot windowless shed, and slipped down to the floor.

"Angie." Jenna's voice was soft. "I want our babies to live."

Angie blinked away hot tears. "Think. We're going to be okay."

Jenna wore a sorrowful expression.

Angie whispered, "Months ago, my daughter's spirit came to warn me about my safety. I know Gigi's going to be born ... and for her to be born, I have to live. We're going to get out of this."

Jenna looked into Angie's eyes. "But, Gigi didn't tell you *I* was going to get out of this."

Angie took her sister's hand. "I'm not leaving you and you aren't going to be hurt."

"Do something," Dave wailed.

Angie whirled to the man. "Hush, you. Your screeching might set off the bomb."

Jenna tip-toed around the space looking for some way to get out while Angie pushed on the door, but it wouldn't budge.

"Is that thing ticking?" Jenna asked with wide eyes. "How much time do we have?"

A metallic whirring sound came from the rectangular box near the door.

"I don't see a timer." Angie asked Dave, "Do you have any tools in here?"

"On the shelf. In the box. What are you going to do? You can't disable a bomb. Don't get us killed."

Angie went to the box on the metal shelf. "If we just stand here and do nothing, that's exactly what's going to happen to us." She lifted two screwdrivers, a pair of pliers, a hammer, and a small crowbar from the container. "The door isn't that sturdy. Let's get it open."

Jenna ran her hand over the door. "The hinges are on the outside, but the door is old and has pulled away from them. If we wiggle the crowbar into the space, maybe we can make it big enough to loosen the door from the hinges."

Dave shuffled his feet across the old wooden floor. "Let me help." He took a quick glance at the bomb and reached for the crowbar. He shoved it into the slit of space at the middle of the door and started to work it.

Angie knelt and used the claw end of the hammer to do the same thing Dave was doing, pulling and yanking to make the door loosen from the hinges.

Jenna used the two screwdrivers to work the door in between where Dave and Angie's tools were positioned.

It must have been over a hundred degrees in the shed and sweat poured off the three people from the combination of fear and the high temperature.

"It's moving." Dave's voice was triumphant. "It's giving way. Keep at it."

Angie could see the space was wider now. *Where was Chief Martin?*

"I think it's loose enough," Jenna told them. "Let's use our weight and try to break the door off."

Angie, Dave, and Jenna lined up side by side with their shoulders facing the door.

"On three," Angie said softly, and then she began to count.

When she got to *two*, the rectangular box near their feet clicked once, loudly. All three of them knew what would happen next.

"Now!" Angie shouted and they slammed their shoulders against the door with such force that the hinges bent and the door opened halfway. "Run!"

Jenna was the first one out and she ran a few yards and turned around. "Come on, Angie!"

Angie was next, running as fast as she could, with Dave at her heels. She grabbed her sister's outstretched hand, and they all took off.

Two seconds later, a deathly sound engulfed them, a blast of burning light flashed, and the shed exploded sending all three of them hurtling into the air and then smashing to the ground.

Debris rained down on them as Chief Martin ran into the yard.

~

"It's a good thing it was an old shed," Angie said to Jenna.

The sisters were sitting on a hospital bed in the emergency room being treated for cuts and bruises.

"You can say that again." Jenna watched the doctor stitch up a slice on her arm. "We cut it kind of close."

"Yeah." Angie gently rested her hand on her abdomen. "But, it didn't matter. We got out."

Chief Martin peeked his head into the room. "Can I come in?" He looked a little paler than usual. "Everyone still okay?"

Angie smiled. "We're all fine. All four of us. Although, two of us will be sore for a few days."

When the bomb went off, the shed was blown up, but thankfully, the angle of the explosion sent most of the wood and nails up and back, away from the escapees. Their injuries were mainly the result of hurtling to the ground.

The babies, though, were perfectly healthy and completely unharmed.

Dave Hanes suffered a broken arm and some cuts, and while he was getting a cast put on, he regaled the nurses and doctors with his tale of his quick-witted escape.

Chief Martin arrived just as the bomb went off and nearly had a heart attack when he saw Angie and Jenna on the ground, bleeding and stunned. Once he saw they were alive, a few tears of joy and relief may have spilled, but he would deny it, if it was ever brought up by anyone.

Within minutes, ambulances, two detectives, police officers, and fire trucks all descended on Dave's house and sprang into action. Joe Boles was found a few miles away and was taken into custody.

Together, Josh and Tom burst into the emergency room while the twin sisters were still on stretchers and when they saw their wives alive and talking, they wrapped the women in their arms.

Shortly after the men arrived, Ellie, Courtney, and Mr. Finch rushed in, and once they saw the sisters with only minor injuries, they were filled with relief and happiness ... and then the teasing and joking started.

"Why do you two have all the excitement?" Courtney smiled. "Couldn't you have brought the rest of us along to get locked in a shed?"

"Miss Ellie might have been able to use her telekinesis skills to bring you a saw," Mr. Finch kidded with them.

Ellie said with a sigh, "I worried you two were in danger. The cats started acting crazy, howling and dashing around the house like maniacs. I called Chief Martin, but he was in a meeting. When he called me back, I was already in the van heading to Dave Hanes's house."

Angie cocked her head to the side and her eyes were soft. "You did? You were coming to check on us?"

"The chief told me to pull over and wait where I was. He was almost to the house."

"I didn't want her walking into trouble," the chief said. "I put the siren on and sped to the house. Unfortunately, a little too late to be of help."

"Chief Martin finally called me and told me you were both okay, but were on the way to the hospital to be checked over. I picked up Courtney and Mr. Finch and we got here as fast as we could." Ellie passed her hand over her eyes. "I can't take much more of this. Please just stay in the house for the rest of your lives."

Courtney slipped her arm around her sister's shoulders and kidded, "My skills must be expanding because I can see the future ... I can see there's no way that's going to happen, sis."

26

The tables behind Mr. Finch's house were laden with all kinds of food, salads of every variety, rice, cut-up fruit, small quiches, pizza rolls, stuffed mushrooms, mini spanakopita, and crackers with ricotta cheese and sliced strawberries. Coolers of cold drinks stood by the tables.

Some of the men were clustered around the grills cooking sausages, veggie burgers, teriyaki chicken kabobs, and garlic shrimp.

Jack, Rufus, Chief Martin, and Mel were playing a game of horseshoes while Lucille, Francine, Mr. Finch, Betty, Ellie, and Jack showed their skill at badminton.

"Oh, my." Betty fanned her face with her hand. "I haven't moved this much in thirty years."

Jenna, Angie, Orla, and Francine's new boyfriend, Bill, were deep into a rousing game of corn hole. Angie groaned when her bag of corn missed the hole and sailed over the platform onto the grass.

Euclid and Circe sat on the Adirondack chairs watching the humans play their games.

Joe Boles was arrested for attempted murder, malicious destruction of property resulting in personal injury, possession of a firearm in relation to a crime of violence, interstate transportation of an explosive, and numerous other charges.

Joe was the man at the hospital who harassed and threatened Carol Leeds. He was the man in the restaurant parking lot who argued and threatened Jesse and Mary Foley. He bore a grudge against Agnes Shield because she wouldn't take his abuse when he yelled and swore at her for getting in the painters' way on the street outside her home and he was infuriated with the Reynolds because they complained about him to his boss.

Joe had it in for Dave Hanes for fighting with him and getting them fired from Blue Sky Painting. Having a certain knack for twisting an event so that, in his mind, he was never to blame for any negative result, Joe believed the people he targeted should be punished for causing him so much distress. Nothing was ever Joe's fault, and was never the result of his own bad behavior.

He delivered the package bombs to Agnes's front porch and to Dennis Leeds's mailbox dressed as a delivery person, ever careful to wear sunglasses, a hat, and to dress in dark-colored chinos and a polo shirt to mimic a company deliveryman.

Joe wore a t-shirt with the Blue Sky Painting logo and company name on it when he got into the alter-cation with Jesse and Mary. The run-in with the young couple was the reason he made a bomb for them which was set to go off when the car engine started.

He was especially proud of his bomb-in-the-log idea which injured Mrs. Reynolds and her teenaged daughter.

Law enforcement discovered a dozen other bombs in Joe's basement along with a list of names of planned targeted victims that included Solana Police Chief Peterson, Chief Martin, the owner of Blue Sky Painting, and Dave Hanes.

Chief Peterson worked with the media to alert people who had ever had an altercation with Joe

Boles to be vigilant about their safety and to call the police if they found anything on their property that might be cause for concern. The police believed that Joe might have bombs already delivered to unsuspecting victims.

Dave Hanes didn't lie about seeing the car at Dennis Leeds's house on the day the bomb was put in the mailbox. Joe Boles owned that car and used it to deliver the package bomb.

When the grilled food was placed on large platters and set on some of the tables, the friends gathered around to serve themselves buffet style and then carried their dinner plates to sit at the picnic tables together. Euclid and Circe were given small plates of plain chicken to eat and both of them were happily chewing away at their feast.

"This was a great idea, Mr. Finch." Angie lifted her fork of greens to her mouth.

"We needed a celebration," Finch said. "Orla and Mel are going to buy my house and Tom will be starting soon on the construction of the Victorian's apartment addition." He glanced at Angie and Jenna with soft, kind eyes. "And all of us are safe and well."

"How is that poor Dave Hanes doing?" Betty piled her plate high with rice, salad, and two chicken kabobs.

Chief Martin answered, "Dave is doing well. His arm is healing and he's making plans to rebuild the shed, but this time he'll include windows on three sides in case he ever needs to make another escape from the structure. With some prodding and encouragement, he also paid a visit to his former boss at Blue Sky to make a case for getting his job back. The boss has agreed to hire him, but Dave must complete a month on probation. If he can make it through the month trouble free, then he will become a permanent employee once again."

"I'm glad for him," Courtney said. "He seems like a decent guy who was tormented at work by a monster. I'm happy he's getting a second chance."

After the meal, a fire was lit in Mr. Finch's portable fire pit and everyone enjoyed dessert and mingled with one another around the yard.

"Your drawings were trying to tell us something all along." Angie kept her voice down.

"If we'd only realized earlier what the pictures were trying to convey to us," Finch said, "things may have been resolved quicker."

"You can't push." Orla joined Angie, Finch, Ellie, Courtney, and Jenna. "You can only interpret the messages we receive whether they are sent visually, orally, or mentally. Information comes in its own way and in its own time. We are merely the receptacles and the receivers."

"It's the interpretation part that's the hardest," Courtney told the woman. "We gather the messages just fine ... usually ... but it's figuring them out that gives us a pain."

"We were slow to pick up on the clues in the drawings," Angie explained.

"Things will get easier as time passes and you gain more experience." Orla gave them all a nod. "How are the mothers-to-be and their babies doing?"

"Good," Jenna smiled. "Angie and I are both past the morning sickness and are doing really well."

"We haven't felt the little ones move yet, but the doctor says it's too early." Angie rubbed at her belly.

"Soon though." Orla nodded. "I know the name you've chosen," the woman told Angie and then looked to Jenna. "Do you and Tom have names picked out?"

"We're working on it." Jenna didn't want to share any possible names just yet. "We haven't found out if it's a boy or a girl, and Tom and I have decided to wait until he or she is born to find out."

"It will be a lovely surprise," Orla said.

Tom and Josh came over to join the group and

the discussion moved from the future additions to the family and furnishing the nurseries, to the weather, the coming end of summer, how their businesses were doing, and the fall festival.

"I'm on the fall festival committee representing the finance board," Ellie told them. "We've already begun our meetings."

"Time flies," Mr. Finch said. "The leaves will be turning colors soon."

Some of the friends decided to return to the games, leaving Jenna, Angie, Orla, and the cats sitting together in the lawn chairs. Euclid rested across Angie's lap, his eyes closing off and on, and Circe had curled up next to Jenna, purring.

"What sweet animals," Orla said, and then added pointedly, "they're very smart, aren't they?"

Angie smiled. "Sometimes, I think they're more than smart."

"Hmm. I wondered about that. They're both very *perceptive.*"

Euclid lifted his head and trilled at Orla.

"Too bad they can't talk," Jenna said.

"Actually, that's probably a good thing," Angie let out a laugh, and then she turned serious. "Jenna and I were talking about our mother recently."

"Oh?" Orla tilted her head slightly to the side.

"She died in Boston. It was a hit and run. Did you know that?"

"I heard about it, yes. I didn't know your mother. I'm sorry that happened to her."

Angie made eye contact with Jenna, and then said, "We were wondering about the accident. It was a clear day on a fairly quiet side street. Why didn't the person slow down when he or she saw Mom crossing?"

"The person must have been distracted," Orla said.

Angie leaned closer. "Do you know anything about what happened that day? Or why it happened?"

Mel's voice boomed across the yard. "Orla, come here and help me. I'm losing this game. I need you."

Orla gave Mel a wave. "I'd better get over there. You know how competitive Mel is."

Angie was about to say something, when Orla looked into her eyes. "We'll have a talk someday soon."

When the woman was out of earshot, Jenna said, "She knows something."

"Yeah. I wonder when she'll tell us."

"Orla said earlier that these things can't be pushed. We'll find out what happened to Mom when the time is right. But for now, I'm going to sit here in Mr. Finch's yard on this beautiful summer evening watching our family and friends ... with two fine felines and my sister right beside me." Jenna reached for Angie's hand and gave it a squeeze. "And think about how lucky we are."

THANK YOU FOR READING! RECIPES BELOW!

Books by J.A. WHITING can be found here:

www.amazon.com/author/jawhiting

To hear about new books and book sales, please sign up for my mailing list at:

www.jawhiting.com

Your email will never be sold, shared, or spammed.

If you enjoyed the book, please consider leaving a review. A few words are all that's needed. It would be very much appreciated.

ALSO BY J. A. WHITING

OLIVIA MILLER MYSTERIES (not cozy)

SWEET COVE COZY MYSTERIES

LIN COFFIN COZY MYSTERIES

CLAIRE ROLLINS COZY MYSTERIES

PAXTON PARK COZY MYSTERIES

SEEING COLORS MYSTERIES

ABOUT THE AUTHOR

J.A. Whiting lives with her family in New England. Whiting loves reading and writing mystery stories.

Visit me at:

www.jawhiting.com
www.bookbub.com/authors/j-a-whiting
www.amazon.com/author/jawhiting
www.facebook.com/jawhitingauthor

SOME RECIPES FROM THE SWEET COVE SERIES

Recipes

FRUIT AND CUSTARD PIE

INGREDIENTS

A little butter to grease the pan

Confectioner's sugar to sprinkle over the pie

2 – 2¼ cups of fruit of your choice – blueberries, raspberries, or seedless red grapes, cherries, blackberries, cranberries

3 eggs

⅓ cup sugar and ¼ cup sugar

⅛ teaspoon of salt

1½ teaspoons vanilla extract

¼ cup heavy cream

1 cup milk

¾ cup flour

DIRECTIONS

Set oven to 375°F.

Butter a 10" baking dish or a pie plate.

Arrange the fruit in the dish.

Using a blender, blend at high speed to combine eggs, ⅓ cup sugar, salt, vanilla, cream, and milk.

Add the flour – blend until smooth.

Pour enough of the mixture to just cover the fruit.

Sprinkle ¼ cup sugar over the batter.

Pour in the rest of the batter and smooth with the back of a spoon.

Bake for about 35 minutes or until the top is puffy and golden, and a toothpick tests the center and comes out clean.

Cool on a wire rack.

Sprinkle with confectioner's sugar.

APPLE CAKE

INGREDIENTS

I stick butter, room temperature

¾ cup sugar

I teaspoon vanilla extract

I¼ cups of all-purpose flour

I teaspoon baking soda

I teaspoon ground cinnamon

Pinch of salt

2 medium-size apples (peeled, cored, and cut into small cubes – can use Honey crisp, Granny Smith, Fuji, or Gala apples or combine two kinds together)

DIRECTIONS

Set the oven to 350°F.

Spray a 9" round cake pan or spring form pan with baking spray; or grease the pan with butter.

NOTE: If not using a spring form pan, it will help to line the pan with parchment paper and grease the top of the paper.

In a large bowl, beat butter and sugar with an electric mixer set on medium speed until fluffy.

Beat in the eggs one at a time.

Mix in the vanilla, flour, baking soda, cinnamon, and salt using low speed until combined.

Using a rubber spatula, stir the apples into the batter.

Pour/spoon the batter into the pan.

Bake for 40-45 minutes or until a toothpick inserted in the center comes out clean.

Cool on a rack for 10 minutes, then remove the cake from the pan to a metal rack and let cool for 10-15 minutes more.

Sprinkle the top with confectioner's sugar.

Serve with the ice cream flavor of your choice or with whipped cream.

Cake may be served warm or at room temperature.

PENUCHE FUDGE

INGREDIENTS

1½ cups powdered sugar

⅔ cup evaporated milk (NOT sweetened condensed milk)

1¾ cups brown sugar (packed)

10 Tablespoons butter, room temperature

¼ teaspoon salt

1½ teaspoons vanilla

DIRECTIONS

Use a 9" square pan; spray with nonstick spray cooking spray; line with plastic wrap.

In a heavy saucepan, over medium-high heat, combine the brown sugar, butter, salt, and evaporated milk; use a long-handled wooden spoon to continuously stir until the butter melts and the mixture begins to boil.

Once it begins to boil, turn heat to medium-low allowing the mixture to simmer; stir frequently for 25 minutes until the fudge forms into a soft ball.

Remove the pot from the stove and place the mixture into a mixing bowl.

Beat in the powdered sugar, a little at a time, until smooth.

Beat in the vanilla.

Pour mixture into the prepared pan.

Use a spatula or the back of a spoon to smooth the top.

Place in the refrigerator uncovered to cool for about 20 - 25 minutes, or until the fudge is firm.

Turn the fudge out of the pan and peel off the plastic.

Cut the fudge into small squares.

SWEET AND SALTY COOKIES

INGREDIENTS

   1¼ cups all-purpose flour

   1¼ cups old fashioned oats

   1¼ teaspoons baking soda

   1¼ teaspoons kosher salt

   2 sticks unsalted butter, at room temperature

   ¾ cup sugar

   2 Tablespoons milk

   2 teaspoons honey

DIRECTIONS

   Preheat the oven to 300°F.

   In a bowl, mix together flour, oats, baking soda, and salt.

With an electric mixer on medium speed, beat butter and sugar until fluffy.

Beat in milk and honey.

Using a spatula, mix in the dry ingredients.

Line a baking sheet with parchment paper.

Spoon Tablespoons of dough onto the baking sheet (space about 1 – 1½ inches apart).

Press down gently to slightly flatten the dough.

Bake until cookies are golden (about 25-30 minutes).

Transfer the baking sheet to a wire rack; cool.

The cookies will become crisper as they cool.

Made in the USA
Monee, IL
24 September 2019